Cameron

FORBIDDEN BOOK 3

KATHI S. BARTON

This is a work of fiction. Names, characters, places, and incidents are products of the author's imagination or are used fictitiously and are not to be construed as real. Any resemblance to actual events, locations, organizations, or persons, living or dead, is entirely coincidental.

World Castle Publishing, LLC
Pensacola, Florida
Copyright © Kathi S. Barton 2018
Paperback ISBN: 9781949812138
eBook ISBN: 9781949812145
First Edition World Castle Publishing, LLC, October 15, 2018
http://www.worldcastlepublishing.com

Cover: Karen Fuller
Editor: Maxine Bringenberg

Chapter 1

Jake tried to read the paperwork he'd gotten this morning about the couple. The man on the bed in front of him had been hurt badly, so critically that it'd taken the nursing staff and doctors twelve hours before he'd been put back together. His sister hadn't fared any better, but she was resting comfortably while Cameron wasn't. He seemed to be jerking uncontrollably and moaning in pain most of the time.

Caitlynn, Cattie to those who knew her, was just down the hall in a private room as well. The bullet that hit her in the back of the head hadn't been as serious as it could have been. They were still working on that, but the man that had brought them to this private hospital said he thought Cameron, Cam to his friends, had called out to his sister which had her ducking. The Hendersons had a great many people looking out for them, and none were human.

"Where is my sister?" Jake stood up, completely forgetting about the paperwork that he'd been working on as it slid to the floor. "I don't know you, do I? Where is Cattie, and my mom and dad?"

"You're at a private hospital for now. Your sister is just down the hall, but I'm afraid she's not able to come in here to see you as yet. As for your parents, your mother — a wonderful person, by the way — is in the cafeteria having a cup of tea with my mate, and your dad was called away. Something to do with his work." The man nodded, then grabbed his head and cried out. "Yeah, they said that you might want to take it easy on moving around too much at first."

Jake watched him struggle with the pain, and the very little that he'd given him in the way of answers to his questions. Jake himself still had plenty of questions, but he could wait.

Cam had been out for several days now, and it had been touch-and-go for both of them since Jake had been called away from his home to help them. Whatever favors had been pulled to keep these two alive had been more than a simple thing, like saving their lives. It had to be so much more than that, he thought, especially since Cam had been critical and Cattie in grave condition when they'd been brought to him. Now they were both on the mend, and it hadn't been that long ago since their first prognoses had been given to them.

"What did you mean that Cattie isn't able to come see me? They were supposed to keep her alive." Jake told the man that the people who had brought her in had done all that they could. "If they'd done what I told them to do, then she'd be up and around, and I'd be wherever she is. Where is Howard, anyway?"

"The man that brought you to me?" Careful this time, Cam nodded. "He told us when we were notified to come and be with you and your sister, that he had to take care of some loose ends. I didn't think he was the sort of man who shared well, so I didn't ask. Would you like to go and see your sister? Like I said, she's doing better, but not as well as everyone had hoped she would."

"Yes. Can I be moved yet?" Jake told him that it was up to him, but he'd take a wheelchair until he was stronger. "All right. You said my mom was close? And with your mate? Is she capable of keeping my mom safe?"

"He. And yes, he's a tiger." Cam said that he was sorry. "No need to be. It's something that everyone does. Forrest, my mate, he said that they're coming up now. And I'm to understand that you have the ability to talk to people, far reaching. I've been told to advise you to hold off on that for a while. They need to see who they can trust here."

"All right." The wheelchair was brought in as Cam's mom and Forrest joined them. Once he was seated, which was not nearly as easy as it sounded, he was taken down the long hall to his sister's room. A couple came out of the room just as they got there. "Cam, these are friends of mine, Henry and Paddy. They've been keeping an eye on Cattie for you. Henry is a wolf."

Cam was rolled right up to the bed when they entered the room. No one said anything to him, but Jake had a feeling that the man was giving a bit of himself to his sister. Howard, the man that had brought them here, had said that Cam was very strong, and stubborn too. Just let him do what he felt that he needed to. Jake looked at Forrest when he came to stand by him. He asked if he'd heard anything more.

"Nothing as yet. I have been reading over the reports on the grocery store." Cam turned to him and asked him what he'd heard. "Just bits and pieces. And your friend, Howard, he's been giving us what he can. I'm not sure, but I think that he wanted to get permission from you before he told us too much."

"More than likely. What did he tell you about me?" Jake told him there really hadn't been much, just that he was an FBI agent, his sister was a cop. "Nothing about what I am? What I can do?"

"No. Just enough to tell you not to reach out to people if you can help it. And that you are very powerful." Jake watched him carefully. He didn't want him to weaken himself more by being out of bed. But Howard had told them that if they took him right away to see her, he might rest easier. "What are you, if I can ask?"

"I'm nothing that you've encountered before. I'm a little of everything, and some of that is pretty nasty shit. About twenty or so years ago, I was hit by a car, completely my fault. The closest hospital was a clinic for shifters. They sort of pumped me up with everything they had in their arsenal to save my life." He didn't say any more, just kept looking at his sister. "I've been on medical leave from the bureau for some time now. They're trying to convince me to come back, but I just don't have it in me anymore. It's overwhelming, being what I am."

"My son is a good boy." Cam smiled at his mom when she spoke. "Both my children are good people. And this thing that brought them here, I'm only just hearing about it. What would you like to know? I can tell you what I've heard from their father, but after that, he'll have to tell you. The store that you were in, it was a set up. Not for you—you were just in the wrong place at the wrong time. But they wanted Cattie gone."

"I figured as much." Jake looked at Cam when he asked him why he'd thought that. "I've been reading over reports of the incident. Most of what I have, its things that not even your police have. A lot of it is from friends I have that can move in and out of places that no one else can. Or so I think. Anyway, Quincey, a vampire, has been looking around as well. He said that your sister, Cattie, knows him."

8

As soon as he said her name, she looked at him. She had the most beautiful eyes, the color of very old emeralds. Jake could see her pain—she wore it as if it were a second skin, one that she'd gladly strip out of. When she glanced at Cam, he could see the resemblance and the love they had for each other. Trust too. Then something occurred to him.

"You're twins." Cam nodded, and Cattie did as well. "You have a bond, too, that others in your situation don't have, don't you? This arsenal you talked about, some of it is in her as well."

"Yes. You're very good. But yes, when I was on the bike, a regular bicycle, she was with me when I was hit. I went up and over the car that hit me and landed on my head. Cattie wasn't hurt, but she didn't leave my side. And because of the bond that we had before, she shared some, but not all of what I got." Cam pushed his chair around so that he could face them. Jake could see that he was mending quickly now, and so was Cattie. "By the time my parents were notified, I had been hurt for several hours. When they got to my side, the damage was already done. As in they had already changed me because of how close I was to dying. I've been laying low since I turned twenty-five. That was when the shit really kicked in."

"Cameron." He apologized to his mom. "You should want to make a good first impression. There is no telling what might have happened to you had these people not stepped in to hide you. But as I was saying, from what we've been able to piece together, they were there to take out Cattie. For what, we just don't know at the moment. But when Cam walked into the store, something that he hasn't done in a while, they decided to take them both out—as far as we can understand, anyway. The robbery was just a ruse to get your sister to the scene."

"I was specially called to hit the store. I was just going off duty when the call came in and my boss told me to go with

9

them. That he'd cover the overtime." Cattie looked at Jake, and he knew that she understood what he'd done. Jake had already seen and talked to the captain of the station through Henry, and his ability to talk to the dead. Shaking her head, she asked him to confirm what he was sure she already knew. "He's dead, isn't he?"

"Yes. Quincey. He said that you'd understand." Cattie nodded. She might understand, but he didn't. "May I ask why they wanted either or both of you dead? I mean, I've been reading over some of the paperwork that was taken from the captain's desk, and he seemed to think you were an all right person. He did have pressure from the higher ups, but that didn't call for killing either of you. I can only assume, and I have a feeling that I'm right, they didn't care for the number of cases that you close. With the help of Cam, I'm betting."

"Yes, that's right. But that was what you were supposed to find." Quincey came in and kissed Cattie on the forehead and shook the hand of Cam. They were both getting better — the cuts on her face were nearly gone, and Cam was standing up now. Quincey handed him another thick file as he continued. "That is curtesy of his home. There is a room that no one found when they were searching his place after he was killed. And to the public, so that you know, he committed suicide. But he's been dirty since before he got out of the police academy. And more than likely before then."

"Why?" Everyone turned to Paddy when he asked the question. "I know a great deal about how a house is run and have even been in on a dirty one or two in my career. But this one, it seemed to be on the up and up without anyone on the take. And believe me when I tell you, I looked hard to find it. There just didn't seem to be anything there."

"For the most part, the majority of the cops were on the up

and up, as you called it. There were only a few, the captain for one, that were dirty. His dirt was going to take down the entire place, sadly. And we think, just from what we've found out recently, that he needed Cattie dead to get her out of the way of something coming soon. Or at least that's what I've surmised so far." Cattie got out of the bed and started stretching and moving around the room while Quincey continued. "But as to why they wanted her dead, I've not been able to find out much more than that she was the target in all this. Sadly, a lot of people lost their lives when the building blew. But their families are being well compensated."

"So, let me get this straight, because this is just too much at once for me." Jake smiled at Forrest when he winked at him. "So, this super cop, Cattie, is a target for some reason. These people, I'm assuming the ones that wanted her dead, are robbing a store to bring her on the scene. I'm assuming that they were going to kill her off, and make it look like she was shot in the line of duty. Then her brother shows up, another super person, and it all goes to shit. But, as far as the public is aware, both of them are dead as well. Correct so far?"

"Yes, but you're missing one important element. No one — no one on her force nor those that I worked with — is aware that I'm anything more than a man who had to take some time off to heal from a job gone south." Jake could see the pain on Cam's face. "I shot and killed a kid. Not that it was an accident — it was him or me, quite literally. When he pointed the gun at me and fired, I returned it, and he was dead and I was shot too. I've been healing since then. It's been about eight months now and I have no intention of going back."

It was so final that no one said anything. Jake could understand it better than most, not wanting to go back to the same thing day after day. Going into partnership, both business

11

and personally, with Forrest had given him a much better outlook on his whole life. And he loved Forrest for it.

~*~

Cam walked the halls of the place they were staying. He'd come to figure out that it wasn't a hospital, at least not now it wasn't. The place had been closed down years ago, but still operated quietly when it was needed. He'd have to ask Howard if they needed any funding to keep it afloat. He knew that without this place, he and his sister would be dead.

There were no other patients in the place but him and Cattie. The staff that was there — very few now — was all in some way involved with keeping the public in the dark about what sort of place it was. Quincey, he knew, now owned not only the building, but also about five hundred acres that surrounded it. Cam came to the conclusion that not only was it not known to the people that were nearby, but they didn't know that there was even a building within the electrified fencing.

"I've been thinking." He smiled at his sister when she came out of the room she'd been in. "Don't say it. I'm really confused about what is going on with my job. I mean, who would want to go to this much trouble to see me dead?"

"You mean besides me?" She punched him in the arm. "I've been thinking on that too. You said that your boss, Captain James, told you to go on this mission, even though you were supposed to be getting off. I wish I could have a long conversation with the bastard to see just how much money he made off of this. And see if hell takes that kind of currency."

"I think we can get that. But you're right, it seemed strange to me, even when the call came in. I mean, we're not the kind of cops that goes out on this sort of thing. We're the ones that go after the scum of the earth, drug dealers, as well as prostitution and counterfeit shit." She looked around to see if their mom was close. Even though they were both in their early thirties, they were terrified of their mom—with good reason. She was their mom, but she had a mean streak in her when they didn't live up to her expectations. "Why did he think that I wouldn't have questioned him about it?"

"Did you?" She said that she had tried, but he was practically shoving her out the door. "I've been thinking on why I was there too. You know as well I do that I don't go out unless it's dire. I mean, being out of lettuce? I haven't any idea why it was so urgent that I go out then. I was thinking that your nervousness of this called out to me in some way, and that's how I ended up there. Even though you didn't contact me, I still felt the need to be with you. I wasn't even surprised that I'd walked into something. Understand?"

"Yes. And so you know, I did think about you while I was waiting on things to be set inside. I was worried about what you'd think of me being there." He nodded and took the turn at the next left. He needed to regain his strength, and this was helping. "So, this thing that we can do—I guess we can add being able to contact each other without contacting each other."

"I'll put that on our to do list." He moved down the hall, her beside him every step of the way. "Cattie, what do you think of the people that are here? The couples. Why them? I mean, it's not like they're anyone we've dealt with before. I've been wondering why Quincey, or even Howard for that matter, had them come to help us."

"Have you talked to Howard yet?" He said that he'd not. "Me either. I did remember seeing him there, when we were taken away, but not much before or after that. Quincey has been telling me for a while now that I need to beef up my own security. I guess he was right."

"Yes, I'd say that he was. By the way, you had a lovely

funeral. Did you see it on the television?" Cattie said that she'd purposely not watched it. "The mayor had so many good things to say about you, though he sort of glossed over me being killed too. I think that the bureau had asked him to do that. I've not tried reaching out to him yet. Have you contacted anyone?"

"No, I'm trying to lay low." They were picking up speed as they came down the next hallway, almost at a jog. "Cam, I have to say, I'm a little worried about Mom and Dad—especially Dad. Did you hear that he got called away last night? Why? The man has been retired for years. Why are they calling him out on jobs after all this time? I have a feeling that it's not work and he's in trouble again."

He knew, but he didn't want to tell Cattie just yet. Cam, too, had been laying low, but he was much better at searching minds than she was, so he had been picking brains for the last several hours.

Cam turned the next corner and came to a sudden stop. There stood Howard. Cam hadn't seen the man in weeks before he'd called to him to come for Cattie. He looked worried, overworked, and closer to his age. The man was ancient, but you'd never know it to see him. The magic of being a vampire had kept him looking much younger than he really was.

"I've some news for you both, but I'd rather wait until the troops are here to listen in too. Jake and Forrest have been taking good care of the two of you?" They both said that they had and asked when they were going to get out of there. "Not for a while yet. I like you both being presumed dead. I think in the long run it will keep you alive longer. What did the doc say about your noodle, Cam? Anything come up?"

"Nope, just as brainy as ever." He had hit his head in the bike accident, and it had been why the people at the clinic had poured all they had into him. His brain—unlike most people,

Cam used every part of it. That was the *magic* that he'd gotten when he'd been hit by the car. "I do have a couple of questions for you concerning the others here. Not anything bad, but I would like to know why them. Why now?"

"I can answer that one for you. You remember Jenna Winslow?" They both said that they did. "She was the long-lost daughter of Quincey. And Jake, he's the grandchild of Jenna, and great-grandson of Quincey. The child that they're raising is half-sister to Jake. The line of familiarity is why he trusts them more than he does even me. And we go back further than anyone I know. Forrest was her attorney and is the mate to Jake. The other two are good friends to them both. That's the connection to all four of them."

"So, Quincey has them come here to take care of us and make sure that—what? We're not killed. Doesn't that put them in harm's way? I'd hate to see them hurt because of this crap." He agreed with his sister, but Howard had more. "They're immortal? Because of their connection to Quincey? I guess that makes sense."

"Quincey told me that up until a few weeks ago, he'd been protecting his grandson, Jake. He kept him in the dark, and those around him, about the fact that he's more vampire than human with some of his magic. As soon as Quincey removed the protection, right after Jenna was killed, he talked to him about it and then took the protection away. Jake has become good with the magic—a great deal of it, I guess—that he inherited from Quincey, but he's still getting used to it. Jake and Forrest both took it fairly well. And the baby sister, she's not all human either." Cam said that was a lot for anyone to take in. "You don't know the half of it, I'm afraid. Jenna, if you recall, had been murdered by her son, father to Jake. Jacob has been sentenced to five life terms for his part in not just his mother's death, but a few other things that had been unearthed by his son. It's a long and terrible story, but you can see where the connection is now."

"Sounds too messy not to be true." Howard nodded at him. "All right. That explains that. But how much longer are we going to have to be hidden away? While I like it here because there aren't a lot of people, I'm going just a little stir crazy. I know that Cattie is as well."

"We need to keep you dead, as I said, for just a little longer. But you'll be happy to know that as of yesterday, there is a track that Quincey had put in for the two of you to run on. And there is equipment that you can use to get some of your strength back in the lower levels." Cam thanked Howard. "Don't thank me, it was Jake. He said that he knew that you two were getting antsy."

By the time Jake and Forrest got there, he and his sister had ordered their lunch. The kitchen here was five-star, Howard told them, and to order whatever they wanted. The magic again, he was told, would get them just about anything they wanted. Cam took them up on that offer and ordered a thick steak and all the trimmings. Cattie did the same, but she ordered pie too. His sister loved the treat. He thought that she might like it better than she did him at times.

They were sitting at one of the large tables in the dining room when Howard came in to have a talk with them all. He had news, none of it good, but it was things that they had to hear. His dad showed up about an hour after the meeting started, and he looked broken. Instead of asking him what had happened, he touched his mind to see what else their father was hiding from them.

His dad had been in trouble before—a great deal of it. While he loved the man very much, he didn't really trust him,

16

and hadn't for a long time. It was just after Cam's last day of work, all those months ago, that he'd begun to see his father in a different light. And had it not been for Cam's intervention, they would have lost their family home, Mom would have been out on the streets, and Dad would have been in prison.

When Dad looked at him, Cam let him. He didn't hide the fact that he didn't want his father around him. He knew that he should have talked to Cattie about him, let her know what he was up to now, but he'd been putting it off for some time now. Cam supposed that he hoped that his father would change. He had, but not in a good way. Orval Henderson was in way over his head, and it was going to get him killed if he didn't get his shit together. And Cam knew that it was going to be next to impossible for him to pay off the debts that he'd racked up, gambling on everything this time—including his children's lives. His dad figured that Cam had gotten him out of it once, and that he'd continue to do so. But he wouldn't. Not again.

Chapter 2

Rick wasn't sure what he was supposed to be doing here. He'd been asked by his buddy and longtime friend, Forrest, to come by his house — that he had a gig for him. Rick hadn't had a gig of any kind for years now and getting a call from Forrest out of the blue, like it had been, couldn't have come at a better time. Pressing the doorbell, he listened to the tune that seemed to echo throughout the house. Beethoven.

Rick and Forrest had grown up together. Not in the sense that they'd been children that had been close. No, they'd figured out that they were gay at the same time, leaning heavily on each other throughout their teenage years and on. Rick had thought himself in love with Forrest at the beginning of their relationship — and in a way, he had been. But not the kind of love that made them "in love," but one that was much stronger and tighter than most married couples had. They were, and would be forever, lifelong friends.

"May I help you, sir?" He grinned at who he thought was the butler. The man looked like he'd been fighting with a dust rag and lost. "We're clearing out one of the large rooms in the

19

barn today, as well as looking for lost treasure. The masters of the house, they're out there now."

"So, I can see. Did you find every cobweb and have it attach itself to you? Or are there more yet that you're looking to find?" The gentleman smiled and invited him in. "I'm Richard Whitehall. I'm here to see Forrest Stout."

"Yes, my lord. He is out in the barn with Lord Winslow. I've only come in to put on some supper for tonight. My name is Walton." He shook the man's hand when he took his jacket. "They've been expecting you. I shall ring down there and see if they're coming up, or if I should send you down. There is quite the do over things right now."

When he was asked to follow him, Rick took the time to look around. Christ, this was a big fucking house. He wondered if they'd bought this house with the intentions of never seeing each other, or if they were planning to invite the neighborhood over to stay with them. Laughing slightly, he followed the older gentleman into the kitchen.

And here was the heart of the house, he realized. There was not just warmth, but also a hominess that he'd not felt in a home, including his own, for a very long time. While Walton made a call, presumably to the barn, Rick wandered through the kitchen to the dining room. He realized his mistake then. The house seemed to warm him like nothing had in a very long time. This house was completely filled with warmth and love. He could see himself living here, if ever given the chance.

"Rick?" He turned when he heard his name. He was hard pressed to tear his eyes from the view out the large window to see his buddy. "You made it. Christ, I've missed you so much. Come on out, I want you to meet my mate, Jake."

They caught up, never that hard of a thing to do between the two of them, as they made their way out to the barn. And when he saw the monstrosity that Forrest had called a barn, he paused in entering the place and smiled at him.

"This isn't a barn. This is a storage unit for every animal ever born — you know that, don't you?"

Laughing, Forrest put his arm over Rick's shoulders and guided him into the barn and out the other end of it. There were no animals in the place, but there were a great many other items.

The place had been used as a storage place for a long time, if the boxes covered in dust were any indication. There were crates that were still sealed up with old straps, and baskets that had lids on them that he'd seen in other countries when he'd been visiting. And there were plastic bags, most of them without as much dust as the rest, but just as neatly put in the large barn.

Rick saw the other man before he saw them. Jake was a good-looking man. Well, it was more than that — he looked like a man that Rick thought he could be great friends with. His smile was easy, his manner of doing the simple task of digging in the dirt was classy. Rick had never thought that he'd consider digging with a shovel as classy, but this man had it in spades. When Forrest said the other man's name, he came toward them with the same ease he had in shoveling. Rick could only see that he was happy, and in love with Forrest.

"You must be Rick. I've heard so much about you." He shook his hand and felt the connection immediately. "I'm only just getting used to this magic stuff, so don't tell me what you are. I'm trying to work it out on my own. You're a shifter. No, that's not it. You're more. An elite shifter, correct?"

"Yes, that's right. Forrest told me that the two of you had gained some extra since you've been together. I love your home. It's beautiful, what I got to see of it." Jake told him that he was staying with them for a while, so he'd get the chance to see it all. "I thank you. But since I have no idea why I've been ordered to come here, let's just play it by ear when it comes to me intruding in your home."

"We have some work that you can do for us. I hope, anyway." No one elaborated, so Rick asked about the digging. "Ah, well, a friend of ours—you'll get to meet them too—can see ghosts, if you can believe that. Anyway, he was talking to one of them, and was told that there is a can of some importance buried back here. We didn't realize until a couple of days ago that this barn was built on the foundation of the one that had been here centuries ago. So, we're having fun trying to find it. But what we have in mind for you is the book Paddy is writing."

Rick looked at Forrest as Jake continued on about the book and the ghost. He wasn't sure what he was supposed to say, but he couldn't help him with the book. He wasn't going down that way again.

Just about five years ago this month he'd been taken apart by the literary world. His book, one about a shifter and his lover, had been a solid hit. Movie deals were being tossed around, and there was talk of some big names wanting the lead part in the movie. Then, an ex-lover had said that he'd written the book, and Rick had stolen his work. It had taken him a great deal of cash to get out from under the lawsuits that were hurled at him. In the end, he'd both won and lost. It was proven that he'd written the book, but he'd lost everything, including his respect as an author, and the movie deals had dried up as quickly as his money had.

"You'll be fine." He looked for Jake and noticed that he'd disappeared. "He went up to the house to see to Jenna, our daughter. And as I said, you'll be fine. Paddy just wants your help in getting his book published, he wants to do it on his own. I thought of you immediately and decided to see if you'd do it.

If you don't, then you're not out anything. We'd love for you to stay with us regardless."

"I can't go there again, Forrest. You of all people know what I had to go through. Even my own father disowned me when that came out. And even though I can't stand the man, he and Mom are all the family I have in this world. Dad acted like he'd had no idea that I was gay and treated me like shit after it was made public." He nodded. "Is your father any better about you? If not, then you have to understand why I can't do this."

"My dad is dead." Rick nearly said good riddance to him, but caught himself in time. "It is good that he's gone. And there was a huge scandal with that too. But as you can see, we all came out on the other end better off."

"I'm so happy for you. You know as well as I that our dads needed to be gone from our lives. And I'm still haunted daily by Dad all the time, and he's not even dead. My dad is in the process of suing me now. He's blaming me for him losing his job about a year ago. He said that the stress of having a gay son had made him take up drinking, when we both know that he was a fucking drunk before this." Forrest said that he was sorry and that he was looking into the lawsuit. "Don't. Please don't. I don't want you to be hurt in this anymore than you have been already. You and my father—he hated you as much as I love you."

And he did. Deeper than brotherly love, and the respect that they had for each other was amazing and unbreakable. Even though years could go by without them speaking to each other, it was easy for them to come together and pick up right where they'd left off. Conversations, sharing, and anything else that they had going on before.

"Hello." Rick turned when the woman spoke behind him, startling her a little. "You must be Richard. I'm Christy. You sure are a big guy, huh? I'm Paddy's sister."

She was beautiful, and so childlike that Rick found himself charmed by just her smile. Christy came to him and hugged him tightly, and for the first time in as long as he could remember, he hugged someone back. When Christy kissed him on the cheek, Rick put his hand over the still warm area and smiled at her. All his stress and everything that he'd been doing lately seemed to just melt away.

"I'm glad that you came to stay with us. I'm not allowed to call myself retarded, but I am. Jake and Forrest are my friends, and they let me hold their little sister daughter." Rick couldn't help it, he laughed. "There it is, a beautiful smile. I knew that you had one someplace. Did you know that you have a ghost with you? She's very glad that you've come here too."

He didn't ask about why she could see ghosts. With the way things were going in his life and those of his friends, if she told him that he had a snail for a nose now, he'd believe her. Besides, she was just too lovely not to believe. He laughed with her.

"So, I have a ghost?" She nodded and told him what the ghost looked like. "That would be my grandma, I think. She's been gone a long time. And I have no idea why I'm all right with you telling me that I have the ghost of my own grandma following me around. Is she well? Is she—I don't know—all right?

"She is well now. And you aren't surprised because you've felt her there with you, haven't you?" He nodded before he could think to lie to her. "She wants you to know that your father is a bastard."

"He is at that, and it's doubtful that he'll change much either. I don't want to be rude, Christy, but are you sure you're seeing my grandma? I mean, has Forrest put you up to this?"

She shook her head and cocked her head as if to listen. Rick had no idea, but he had a feeling she was listening to his grandma. "What is she telling you?"

"She said to tell you that you're a grown assed man, and to pick up your pouty lip and get going on helping these men." Christy laughed, and he did as well. It sounded so much like his grandma that he knew without a doubt to believe her. "I think I like your grandma. She said to tell you that she couldn't help you before—there wasn't anyone to help her speak to you. But now that you're here, she expects you to talk to her whenever you can."

Tears filled his eyes and his heart hurt for the words. Not because she'd said them, but for the reminder that they gave him. Rich had not gotten back in time to see his grandma before she passed away, and it had hurt him more than he could have told anyone. But this young woman had not only put him in touch with his grandma but had made him laugh several times in just a few minutes.

"I missed her funeral." Christy nodded. "I swear that my father did that on purpose. He didn't want me to come home and be with her when she passed. I've never forgiven him for that. And I won't."

"She said to tell you that he did that to you, but it's all right now, you're both together. And she says that your father won't win against you in this thing he's doing. Your grandma, Crystal, said that she might be dead, but she has friends in all the right places for you." Again, he laughed, and hugged her when she put her arm through his. "The rest of them are at the house now. Then later we're going to go and see some people that are very special. I love them both."

She talked to him about what she'd been doing as they made their way to the house. Forrest was behind them, interjecting when he could about this or that. Forrest told him that he couldn't wait for him to meet Jenna. And that dinner was going to be late because of a few things that Henry and Paddy were up to.

The house was full by the time he came back down from his room later. He'd been given a suite of rooms on the second floor, so nice that he might not ever want to leave the house. The house, all of it, had charm and happiness in it that he'd missed since his grandma had passed. Not that Rick had had much of that when he'd been younger, but here, he thought that he could get used to it. Paddy and Henry were just as wonderful as he'd thought they'd be, and dinner was not just loud, but fun too. Rick hadn't had this much fun in a very long time.

Henry came to talk to him about his grandma after they ate. And he also told him about the movie that he was going to be in. Paddy was writing a book about a family he'd met when they'd found a trunk in the attic of their home. They were all busy, and it didn't seem to matter to the people they were working with that they were gay men. If this kept up, these little glimpses of stories, Rick thought that he might need a scorecard, or at the very least some way to keep it all straight.

"Currently, we're keeping an eye on a brother and sister for Quincey. You'll meet him later tonight. He said that he had to go home for a couple of days to straighten out some business." Rick said that he had heard of him from Forrest but didn't know him. Jake nodded. "You'll like him. He's a no-nonsense sort of person, but not rude. He's my grandda. Well, great-grandda."

"Forest told me. And I'm sure that I will like him too. How long have you guys known each other? It seems like you've been friends for a long time." They all laughed, and he thought that he'd said something funny. "This is going to be good then, I'm betting."

"Nope. We've just met, actually. Forrest and I met when I needed an attorney. My ex-wife was a nut ball, and he helped me get a divorce from her. We fell in love almost from the start. Then a few weeks later, Forrest called another friend of his, and Henry came out to stay, where he met Paddy. So, Paddy and Christy became family." Jake seemed lost in thought. "I guess we've been friends for about four months now. Doesn't seem that short of a time, you're right. We became the best of friends from the very start."

When he made his way up to his rooms for the night, Rick felt lighter than he had in ages. Not sure where his grandma might be, or even if she was with him, he told her goodnight and that he loved her. Almost as soon as his head hit the pillow, he was asleep. Another thing that he'd not had in a long while was a good night's sleep. He felt he was going to get it tonight.

~*~

Cattie ran the four-mile trek three times before she finally had to quit. She felt better than she had in ages, thanks to getting enough rest, good food, and having her brother right there where she could see and talk to him. He was depressed, she knew that, but she hoped that with getting out and about, he'd feel better soon. She loved Cam more than she did anyone in the world.

"Hey." She stopped her cool down and looked at the man coming toward her. He was in track clothing and was sweaty, but she didn't know him, and trust wasn't high on her list of things to give a stranger yet. When he stayed where he was, she reached behind her and pulled her gun out to where he could see it. "I'm Richard Whitehall. I'm a friend of Forrest and Jake. You know them."

"I do. But that doesn't extend to knowing you. How did you get in here?" He pointed to the gate that she'd come through, but she didn't turn to look. "I'd very much like it if you were to raise your hands above your head and turn around for me. I want to see if you're armed."

"I'm not, but okay." He did just what she wanted him to do, and she didn't see a weapon on him. "Henry said that I could come here and run. I have to run daily or I get a little stiffened up. You must be Caitlynn Henderson."

"Yes." She still didn't trust him, and he seemed to be all right with that. "My brother and the others, they know that I'm out here. So, if you mean any harm to any of us, you'll be dead if you even try."

"I'm aware of that. If you were to reach out to your brother, he's with Jake and Forrest now. They can tell you who I am and what I'm doing here." Cattie wasn't reassured when he knew just what names to say. She didn't care who he knew—he was still a stranger to her. "I'm not going to come any closer, I promise. Just ask them so that I can finish my run, please. I wasn't kidding when I told you that I get stiffened up when I'm not busy."

She reached out to Cam. He was laughing when he answered her. *I was just talking to Jake about you and Rick meeting. Is he still able to get up and around? I've not met him yet, so if you could hold off shooting him, I'd appreciate it.*

Fuck you, you shithead. This man shows up out of nowhere in a place that we've been told is off limits to everyone outside of our little circle. What I should have done was shoot first, then ask you afterwards. Cattie told Richard that he could run. She made her way to the benches at the side of the track. *Who is this guy? Some friend of the family, no doubt. But he doesn't look like the type that would hang out with your sorry ass.*

As I said, I've not met him, but he's here to help out with the book that Paddy is writing. How much longer are you going to be out there? They want to take us to their house for dinner tonight, and since I'm equally as sick of your company as I'm sure you are mine, I told them we'd go. She said that she had to get a shower. *Okay, that's good. If you could tell that guy with you that we'll be ready in an hour, we can get out of here for a little while.*

Cattie told Rick, what he said to call him, that they were going to dinner at Jake's house when he rounded the track again. He nodded and said that he had one more round to go, and then he'd be ready. Cattie watched him run. Whoever he was, he was one serious runner. She'd bet that he did marathons too.

After a long, hot shower, she dressed and made her way back up to the floor she and Cam had been staying on. Today was the first day that she'd been out alone, and it felt good. Cam was right — they were getting sick of each other's company, and she needed to get out a little more.

She had come to love being around the other men — all of them, including Quincey, who made her feel like a queen. And he had been nothing but polite. Kind to her, as well as comforting. Just last night he'd brought her a dozen of the most beautiful roses that she'd ever seen. A girl could get used to this sort of treatment.

When she joined them in the room her brother had taken as his own, she asked him how much work he'd gotten done on the projects that they were working on. Quincey had asked them to look into the deaths of the two men that had been outside the store when it went up, and to find out what, if any, involvement they might have had in the robbery. She could account for the two in the back — she'd killed them both when Cam was helping her. But, according to Cam when he reached out to see what he could find, no one seemed to remember seeing the two in front.

"I've been busy while you were trying to kill some of our newly acquired friends. I was just telling them that these two men aren't anyone." She knew what he meant—they were not in the systems, nor had their fingerprints shown up anywhere. They were just nobody until they could figure it out. "What did you find out about the car that was left on the lot?"

There had been six cars on the lot when the explosion had gone off. Four had been the employees', one was the getaway car, or so they had thought, and the last one was unaccounted for. They had been, under the radar, looking to see who it might have belonged to. They thought that it would go a long way in trying to figure out who was in charge of the hit on her. All she'd been able to find out was that the car was a rental, but she was narrowing that down too.

"The rental agency said that the person who rented it did so online. It was paid for two days before it was ready for pick up. They have this deal where if you don't want to stand in line, you can do it all online. The person whose name was on the paperwork is a woman by the name of D. H. Smith." She handed him what she had on the name. "She's been dead for about six years, according to the records at the nursing home. The phone number that they had for her is a dead end. I can't even find anything more about the woman, nor her stay in the nursing home. She was taken there, then died there sometime later."

"Who is D. H. Smith? I mean, other than a dead woman." She told Paddy what she'd been able to figure out about her. "So, they figured that she had no children, no relatives left at all, and the nursing home where she was staying doesn't know anything about her either. I wonder why no one claimed her. I mean, how did she get to the hospital in the first place, and why?"

"No, apparently she was a Jane Doe when she hit the hospital, but the nursing home changed her name to Dead Human Smith fourteen when someone showed up for her. I guess they get those from the city, those type of people, and they give them names as to what they are, then the number to account for which one. The man before her that was brought in was Dead Human Smith thirteen. He'd been brought in a few weeks before, and died only a few days later, before DH fourteen did." She handed him the paperwork that she'd gotten that morning. "Also, and this is really strange, about a week before she died, someone came in to visit her. They don't have a sign in system, so they just show up and leave, I guess. They weren't there long, but when the visitor left, they had to change the bedding she was in. Apparently, the visitor had gotten ink all over the bed and her hands."

"So, they had her prints to use someplace else." Cattie told Paddy that's what she thought as well. "Were there any prints of hers in the car?"

"I don't know. The car, along with a lot of other things that were in the car, was torched. Torching that had nothing at all to do with the store. It happened the day after the place went up." Cattie was a good cop and enjoyed narrowing down things like this. Her brother did as well. She was also enjoying bouncing ideas off Paddy and Henry too. "The car had been towed away. Not to the rental agency as you'd think but taken to a lot and crushed. That's why it's becoming a little harder to trace it. I guess the paperwork on the car is missing too. Go figure."

"Weirder and weirder. What did the report say at the station? Have you been able to get into those files?" She told her brother that she hadn't been able to. Someone was fucking with the password program. "So, we have a dead woman that somehow showed up driving a car to a store, and when it didn't get destroyed by the bomb that went off, someone took it upon themselves to go and take it so no one could study it."

"Not only that, but the paperwork that I'd gotten from the nursing home has come up missing. I had made copies of everything in her file before sending it back when they asked for it. Something about an insurance claim. When I called back yesterday to see who the insurance company might be and who they were representing, they told me that the file was missing. They had that I'd turned it in, but it was gone now." She handed them the receipt of the file. "As you can see, I'm Margaret Cunningham on the paperwork. But when I called back, I swear the man called me Ms. Henderson. He said that he'd messed up and had the wrong name. I cut ties with that place immediately."

"So, they might know that you're alive." Cattie shrugged at Henry's statement. "I'd bet on it now. I'll look into some of the people that I know around town, see what they might really know."

Cattie looked at her brother and waited. He'd be in and out of the minds of everyone that worked there before she could make a single call. He looked at her and nodded. They did know she was alive, and that could be really bad.

"We need to get out of here. If they know that I'm alive, then it'll only be a matter of time before they realize that Cam is too. And while there are just a handful of people that know what he can do and what he is, we need to get gone before they come here." Jake said that they'd not get here. "Are you willing to bet my life on that? Or that of your daughter, since you bring her here too? I'm not."

"All right. I'll talk to Quincey and see what he wants to do. I would like for you to stay at our home, but that'll be up to him. He knows the extent of extremeness that we've gone through to make the house safe. I'm sure that he'll agree that you'll be the safest there."

When they loaded up to go to Jake and Forrest's home, she rode with her brother. Cattie wanted him close so that she could protect him. And even though he was a bigger threat than she was, she needed to know that he was as safe as she could make him, even if that meant taking a bullet for him. Her brother meant the world to her, as she was sure that she did to him. Nothing would come between them, ever. And she knew for sure that he would say the same about her.

Chapter 3

Cam loved the old house. The fact that they had all the room of a large hotel only made it better for them to be staying there. He would have one like this someday. While he had a large place, it wasn't a home. Not yet. When he'd get around to that, he had no idea, but he wanted everything this one had — the comforts, the love, and the companionship. He made his way around the first floor before heading to the kitchen. He needed to get something to drink before dinner, and they'd said that there was plenty of juice there. Juice sustained him better than anything else. He supposed because it was all natural.

The man standing in front of the fridge looked like he had been there a while. He was leaning against one of the double doors, and it wasn't until he spoke that Cam realized that he was talking to someone on the phone. He quietly sat down to wait, not at all thinking that he might be intruding. The man didn't seem to know he was there anyway.

"Yes, I understand what you're telling me, Father. But you can also bet that I don't give a shit. You're the one that brought this on yourself. I can't help it if you are now getting blackballed by your customers. If you asked me, I'd say that they should have been doing this long before now. Like I said to you, I don't really give a shit what happens to you anymore." The man sighed heavily but didn't move away from the door. "No, actually, I really don't give a rat's ass how you're feeling, either. As I have said to you many times, even in this one call, I really don't care. And I'm not bailing you out any a second time. I have money for me, not to get you out of debt, again."

The man turned then and saw him there. Cam returned the greeting when he waved at him, and nearly swallowed his tongue when the man sat down across from him. Christ, he was really good-looking, and big. As he continued the one-sided conversation, Cam got up and made himself a glass of juice. He also poured the stranger one before sitting again. He had a feeling he knew who he was but wasn't one hundred percent sure. When their fingers touched, it was like he'd been set on fire, the heat of him burned so badly. He stared at him for several seconds, and the whole time he could hear the man on the other end of the phone screaming at his son to help.

"Dad, I have to go. And if you're really smart, which we both know that you're not, you'll lose this number. I'm not going to talk to you again." He closed the phone that had been next to his ear while the man on the other end was still talking. The man sat there quiet for several minutes before he shook his head and smiled. "I'm Richard Whitehall. You must be Cameron Henderson."

"Yes, but I go by Cam." Rick, as he'd heard he wanted to be called, just sat there. It took Cam a few minutes more to realize what was going on between them. He stood up, and so did Rick. "I should go."

"No, you shouldn't. I think it's a bit late for that now anyway, don't you?" He nodded and sat down. "Please tell me that you're not married to that beautiful young woman down the hall."

"That's my sister." Cam heard him say good, or something like that. "I'm not sure what to think about anything. I mean, what I am thinking might not even be close to what you're talking about."

"Okay, fair enough. I'm thinking that you being my mate could be the worst thing at the moment that could be happening to either of us. Not terrible, just bad timing. What were you thinking?" He nodded. "Yeah. Just what I thought. How are you feeling about this? I'd really like to know."

"I haven't any idea or thoughts on it either way. You?" Rick said that he didn't either, not really, just bad timing. "You keep saying that. What about it is bad timing for you? I have a list of reasons as well, but we can go over yours first if you'd like."

"As you heard, my father is making it difficult for me. While Jake and Forrest are helping me out with that, I'm helping Paddy with his book. You?" He told him that he'd been hurt recently when someone tried to kill his sister. "Oh, so nothing out of the ordinary for you either."

They laughed, and Cam felt a lot better. "I'm not human. You aren't either, correct? Elite?" Rick said that was right. "I'm a bit of everything, as I've told the others, but I'll elaborate if you wish."

"Yes, but not now. I want to get to know you for sure, but I think we both have things to work out. Such as parents. Do you have any?" Cam told him that he had a mom and dad, and his dad was in trouble too. "My dad gets started on things, like Ponzi scams, and doesn't think it won't work for him. He's forever an optimist, while throwing away money like he has an unlimited supply of it. Which he doesn't, not anymore. Then he expects me to come to his rescue before he has to go to jail. I should have let him go a while ago, but he's my dad, no matter how much I dislike that fact."

"My father is a gambler. He's done it before, gotten in over his head. He's not any good at it, but it doesn't stop him from doing it. My mom threatened to leave him a long time ago, but she still hangs on to the hope that he'll change. She held him back on a great many things, according to my dad. But here lately, he's been coming around trying to get me to pay off his debt too. Or my sister. Who, by the way, has a great deal of ready cash. I do as well, but I'm not giving it to my father. Like you, not again." Rick nodded and sipped his juice. "Why are you upset about helping with Paddy's book?"

"Not upset, but I've had some trouble before." Cam asked him if he thought that Henry would screw him over. "No. Not him—not ever him. But I do worry that once he does get his book out there—and from what I've read, it's fantastic—but I'm worried that someone will somehow find out I helped, and that might be bad for him."

"Richard Whitehall. I remember now. You had this guy say that he wrote the book and you were taking it from him, or something like that." Rick told him that was it precisely. "Okay, I can see your issue with it. But I don't think you have to worry about that from him. Henry is getting this straight from the ghost's mouth, I heard."

"Yes, he is." Rick laughed. "You always this positive? If so, I might need to have you tone it down a bit if you're like this before I've had my tea. Which is what I drink instead of coffee."

"I'm not usually, no. Tea? I guess I could drink that. I'm not much of an anything drinker, to be honest. Well, water. Sometimes when I'm feeling a little low on energy, I have a gallon of juice." Rick said that was his favorite go to as well. "I'm a semi-retired FBI agent. I had some trouble about a year ago and I shot a kid. He was seven and fired at me first. It took its toll on me a great deal. Then it got to the point where I was enjoying being alone. I can feel people."

"Feel, as in emotions? I can do that too, to a point. Read minds as well. Also shift. That takes the most out of me." Cattie came into the room then and asked if she could join them. Cam looked at Rick, and when he moved over on the bench seat, she sat down next to him. "Your brother and I are getting to know each other. We're mates."

Cattie was never one to get emotional about much. About him, sure, and her job, but nothing that she couldn't control. So, when she took a big drink of her iced tea and set it down, Cam was almost afraid of what she might say. When she put out her hand to Rick, he took it without hesitation.

"Welcome to the family. However, you hurt him, you're dead. I'm just laying that out there for you." Rick looked at him then back at Cattie. "I'm a good shot too. And most of the time have silver in my gun."

Both of them burst out laughing. Cattie hugged them both and told them that she wasn't kidding about hurting him. Cam waited to see what Rick would say, and when he reached over and took his hand in his, it felt right, like a connection was made between the three of them. And he was fine with it.

~*~

"Where the hell is she if not dead? And that brother of hers? Where the fuck is he hiding out in all this? I'm telling you right now, Wayne, if she shows up at the drop point, I'm fucking going to kill you all. This is the most important shipment we've ever gotten in, and you can't find the one person, the single-minded one person that can fuck it all to hell and back for us." Wayne didn't so much as blink at him. Dalton was as pissed as he'd ever been about something, and his right-hand man looked like he'd been dipped in concrete. He just might be before this was all done. His thinking was, being an agent, as they both were, should give them some heads up. But so far, they had nothing but guesses on everything about Caitlynn. And that wasn't working out so well.

"We do know that she's out there. She's been making inquiries around town about the blast and the robbery. That was a major fuck up. I told you it would be, and you didn't listen. So, if you're planning to place blame for that one on me, you can just stop right now." It was tempting. Tempting as fuck for Dalton to reach into his pocket and pull out a gun. He wanted answers to his questions, not someone placing more shit on his oatmeal. "She doesn't know, if that helps, that we're aware of her still kicking around. I will let you know when I have shit to tell you. Not before. And stop fucking calling me in here every day to ask me the same questions over and over. I don't fucking know where she is."

Dalton Carter didn't like being spoken to that way. Hell, his own mother never spoke to him that way. But this man was helping him become a millionaire—perhaps even more than that, but he wasn't aware of that yet. And Dalton planned to keep it that way. As far as Wayne was concerned, there wasn't going to be any money made on this first of many deals because it was a trial run. It was, in a way, a trial run for the moron across from him.

"What about her brother? I know that he was this big prick with the Feds. Where is he? Any clues with that one?" Wayne just stared at him. "Do you have any, I don't know, fucking clue what will happen to us if either of them show up? I mean, do you have any idea how much time we'll spend behind bars, if we even make it that far? They're too good, too smart for us to not be concerned with. I don't know what it is they have—a fucking hand to God for all I know — but she's been dicking in my shit for too long."

"I don't know where he is. Last I heard he was in the aftermath of that robbery gone wrong too." If he reminded him once more about that, Dalton was going to do something he might or might not regret. "The really fucked up part of that whole thing is, there were bodies to account for them being there — a man and woman blown up to nearly nothing. We all assumed, you included, that it was them. If it wasn't, who the hell helped them out with that?"

Something that had been bothering him as well. At least she had people in high places. More than likely her fucking brother did as well. Why? Who was helping them out? From what he'd gotten from her boss, she was just lucky. For some reason, after this, Dalton wasn't buying that. They had someone on the inside of his crew. And once he found them, he was going to rock their little world until there wasn't even a drop of blood to identify them. Christ, this was so bad, he didn't even know where to begin, he was so afraid of her.

"Six weeks ago, we had this all set up. Six weeks of putting men in the right places. Paying off people to have this thing go as planned. And on the day that it's to go down, not only did both of them disappear — because we both know that he's out there too — but the fucking place went up like it had had enough explosives to take out an entire neighborhood. Well, it did, but we're no closer to figuring this out than we were before." Again, Wayne just sat there, like he was one of the living dead or some bullshit. "Are you even aware? I mean, of life in general? Are you clued in? Do I need to get something to make you see what kind of shit we're in?"

"I know just exactly what sort of shit we're in. But to be honest with you, once again, I told you to wait until we had better intel on the two of them." Dalton counted to ten. Then ten more, just so he could breathe properly. He could swear that his gun was just vibrating to get out of his pocket and be used. "We're going to be fine."

"And how on earth did you come to that conclusion? Do you have some sort of crystal ball? Perhaps you've had your fucking palm read? How do you even fathom that this is anywhere close to us being fine about any of this?" Wayne said that he had it covered, and that he knew that they were going to be all right. "Oh well, then let's make some more plans. How about if we have another train load of guns go across four states, only to end up in a police lock-up. Sure. Sure. I can see where you'd think that. Because you want to know why? You're a fucking moron, that's why. Mother fuck, I can't believe that I ever thought we'd be able to work together."

"You worry too much." Dalton pulled out his gun and laid it on the desk. "You use that and you'll never find out what I know."

"Last I heard, you didn't know shit." Wayne told him that he knew plenty. "About what? And were you going to share this kernel of information, or did you think that I'd not need to know?"

"You do, but since you've been ordering me around like I have to be led around by my dick, I decided that I'd hold off until you're in a better frame of mind. And since it doesn't look as if that is ever going to happen, I thought that I'd share now. We shot her in the back of the head. I did, as a matter of fact. And when I was coming out of the building, I made sure that her brother was shot in the head as well. That didn't work out so well, but even if she's out there, she's not in her right mind."

This time Dalton did the staring. Did he not just say that she'd been hunting around about some of the shit that had been going down? That, to him at least, didn't sound like a woman with brain damage. Didn't even sound to him like anyone that had been hurt at all. Instead of pointing out these glaringly stupid comments, he just asked Wayne how he'd come to that conclusion.

"Look, for all we know that might not have even been her. Who the hell would even be able to be up and around after I personally shot her in the head? No one, unless they're a wizard, and I really don't think she's even close to being that. What if — and this is just the way my mind thinks — what if she had some little pissant of a subhuman doing this before she was shot? What if — and here is where it starts to fall together — she had this same pisser looking stuff up before all this went south, and he's not been told if she's coming back or not?" Okay, Dalton could see that happening. If he didn't keep up on his men every day, they'd keep doing the same shit every day and wasting time. "So, this little pisser, he's out there just plugging along and doing what she last assigned him to do. And you remember the reports we got back on her? She's a ball buster, a pain in the ass, and one for details. Like I said, we have nothing to worry about. Not, at least, until we actually see her."

"All right. Then how do we find this person? And I'm not saying that you're right. I'm just wondering if, in all your thinking and plotting, you figured out a way to make this person stop fucking around in our business." Wayne asked him why it mattered. "What do you mean? Of course, it matters."

"Who is he going to report to? You? Not likely. His boss? Nope, dead as she might be. Perhaps someone over her head? Not going to happen either. This person works for her and knows her temper. He or she is going to just sit on it until someone comes to ask for it. And that just isn't going to happen anytime soon. Right?"

He was making sense. And so was what he was saying. If she'd had someone working for her, then that would be, sooner or later, a dead end too. And he had seen her go down — the blood on her face was profound. And the brother? Hell, if he had any sense, he'd be laying low and trying his best to not get dead like his sister. Yes, this was making him feel better about a great many things. But he wasn't going to let this bastard know it.

After a bit more conversation, none of which he paid that much attention to, Dalton was left alone to get some other shit done. He had two bodies to dispose of today — one of them his ex-wife, the other a former partner that had tried to fuck him over.

He'd actually gone to the Feds and told them that Dalton worked for someone in the underworld. Good thing for him that he had contacts in the federal realm, or he might be singing out other names to get himself out of trouble. As it was now, Dalton had three large notebooks, all in code, with the information he needed to take out even the worst of the worst. He hoped never to have to use it, but it was there, ready for him should he need to. And he didn't think he'd be the least bit squeamish about it either.

"You end up owing me something, then you're going to be fucked over by me. I don't fuck around." He looked at the list of things that he needed to get done today, the bodies first and foremost. Dalton picked up the phone to make a clean-up call as his daughter came flouncing into the room like she owned it.

"Daddy, I need money." He didn't say anything. If he pissed her off, he'd have to give her more to shut her up. "I was looking at my closet, and there just doesn't seem to be anything in there that I like anymore. Do tell me that I can upgrade my wardrobe before winter season comes. It's only six months away, you know."

"Perhaps if you had kept up with the exercise program that you'd been on, then your wardrobe would still look good on you." As soon as the insult left his mouth, he knew that he was in trouble. Debra's lower lip pouched out, then it started to quiver. "I'm not saying that you're fat, honey. But you're as out of shape as your old man is. We should take long walks together."

Too late. There was no salvaging this once she started on the tears. Dalton just waited, counting to ten several times before he just pulled out his wallet and handed over his credit cards — four of them. And he'd bet any amount of money that by the time he was ready to go to bed, they'd be so maxed out, he'd have to ask for an extension on paying them back.

Her mother had been the same way, always pushing him to the limit of his endurance with money. Damn it all to hell, couldn't just one woman in his life just say, "No thanks, you don't have to buy me off to keep me happy? Just being with you is enough." Like that was ever going to happen.

Once Debra was gone, her loud sobs still echoing through the main hall, he picked up the phone once again. Someday, he was going to have to take care that he was alone again. Kids and wives were the ruination of the fucking world.

"I need to have some dry-cleaning picked up before five today." The woman on the other end asked him for a code. Once he was able to unearth it on his desk, he gave it to her. "Can I get a rush on that? I'm due someplace tomorrow."

"Yes, but it'll be an extra charge on that for you. If you want them to be perfectly clean." He said that he did and told her thanks. "No reason to thank us, Mr. Smith. We're here for you."

Sure you are, he thought as he hung up the phone, *so long as my check or credit card clears, you'll be Johnny on the spot for me.*

Otherwise, I'd be having to clean up this mess on my own. Not that he'd not done it before, but he was a man that didn't bother when the mundane anymore and getting rid of bodies was that. Not to mention, difficult to get done with a house full of servants and family.

Dalton decided that tomorrow he was going to do something for himself. There were a couple of things that he wanted to get taken care of, the banking first of all. Then he might get him a suit, as well as a lovely dinner with one of the women from his stable of them. Yes, he thought, he'd treat himself to a good fucking, dinner, and a suit. Not necessarily in that order, either.

"Soon I'll have this other shit taken care of, then I can move on with things. I'm going to marry off Debra, first and foremost, just to get myself in with some other groups of men such as myself." He was clicking off notes to himself as he gathered up his phone and wallet and called for his car. Yes, this was going to be epic, as soon as things started to fall into place with that fucking bitch.

He hoped so, anyway—for everyone's sake. If she didn't go down, dead in other words, then there were going to be a lot of people that were going to take her place. He'd see to it. And that fucking Wayne Leon? He'd be at the top of the list too.

Chapter 4

Cam was on the track in the sublevels of Jake's home. It was great to be here and have everything he needed. It wasn't like he couldn't afford a gym membership, or even the best foods if he wanted them. But this was a way to recoup and to relax.

Cam glanced over at his sister when he noticed that she was sitting on the rowing machine. "That works better when you actually work with it." She flipped him off. "Well, you're in a good mood. What has your panties in a twist? Anything I can help you with?"

"Dad called me." Well, there wasn't any need for her to say much more, so he moved to sit next to her on the bench. "He said that you told him you were going to pay off his debt, and he wants to know if he can hang at my house while you get things straightened out. Please tell me that you didn't agree to help him again."

"I didn't. He's playing you. What did you say about him staying at your home?" She just grinned. "Yeah, I'm betting that went over as well as it did when he asked me for some walking around cash—which turned out to be about fifty grand. What sort of walks do you suppose he's taking if he needs that much cash?"

"Not the kind of walks I want to be on. How the hell did he think that was even going to work?" He told his sister that he had no idea. "Yes, me either. He's such a nudge, don't you think?"

"I can think of better words than a nudge, but yes, he's all that and more. What did you tell him about any of what is going on here?" She said that she'd not told him anything. "I was thinking about that too. How did he know that our houses were empty? Is he going by them on a regular basis to see if he can get in? And here's something else—how did he find out that neither of us were dead when the rest of the world thinks we are?"

She looked at him, shocked. He wondered if anyone else besides him had thought of that. Cattie sat there for a few more minutes, sort of half attempting to row a bit. When Rick joined them, wearing a pair of jogging pants and nothing else, he asked him what he thought of his ideas about his dad.

"You know Henry?" They answered that they did know him. "Okay, well, he's got this ghost that does things for him— his name is Wally. I guess he can pop in and out of places, and no one is the wiser. Anyway, he was just at my dad's house. Not his house, really, but this hotel that he's been skipping out on the money for. He went there, found out that my dad is in for a lot of money, and was even able to tell me what he was wearing. He also was able to swipe his cell phone."

"You think he'd do the same for us?" Rick got up on the treadmill and shrugged and told Cattie that he didn't know why not. "All right. I'll go and talk to Henry now. You two should work on the kinks of your relationship. The tension is so tight that a person could walk on it. I'll see you both later."

Cattie was forever his best friend, but there were times when he'd just as soon tape her mouth closed as to hear what she had to say. He loved her, but damn it, she had to know that they were both a little tense about this new relationship. Cam told Rick that he was sorry for his sister's mouth.

"She does cut to the point of something, doesn't she?" Rick was setting the treadmill up with a program. It was the same one that he used, he noticed. "I was thinking about a couple of things about us. And you can say no. Like we both have said, we want to get to know each other a little more before we jump into bed."

"I've never had sex before." Rick nearly fell off the treadmill when he stopped to stare at him. "I've been...I guess you could say that it's too much for me to touch someone. I mean, I had some fun before this thing happened to me, but since then, it's too much. I cannot just feel what they're feeling, but I become as emotional and as overwhelmed as they are too. And I've noticed that women and men have the same emotions, as far as I can tell. They're, for the most part, too greedy, and that made me feel the same way, and nothing ever came of sex other than the first touches. I can't distance myself from their feelings so that I can enjoy sex, or any other kinds of heavy emotions. Am I making the least bit of sense?"

"I think what you're trying to tell me is that you can't concentrate on your own enjoyment when you're getting wrapped up in your partner's. Right?" Cam told him that was it precisely. Rick stopped the mill and came to sit next to him — not touching, but just sitting there. "When I held your hand the other day, what did you get out of it? I mean, did you feel what I was feeling, or nothing at all?"

He had to think about it. And while he was thinking about what he'd felt or even thought, Rick took his hand into his again and told him to tell him what he was feeling. "Nothing. What I mean is, I don't feel anything coming from you. No selfishness. No greed. All I can feel from you is the warmth of your hand in mine and how good it feels."

"Okay. You might think this is insane, but now you touch me." He wasn't sure what he wanted and told him that. "I'm the one that came to touch you. I took your hand into mine. You touch me."

"Okay. But can I touch you anywhere?" His cock stretched in his loose-fitting shorts, and he had to move around on the bench until he wasn't hurting himself. "What I mean is—"

"I know what you meant, Cam. But yes, you can touch me anywhere or any way you want. Just remember, I get to do the same to you." Cam didn't know what that might mean. To him it sounded like a positive sort of threat. But he reached out and touched Rick on the cheek, running his hand over his stubble down to his chin, then up again to his ears and over them. "What, if anything, are you feeling? And if you tell me nothing, I'm not going to believe you. I can see the outline of your cock through your shorts."

"I'm feeling—I'm not sure what you'd call this, but all I can think about is touching you." Rick ran his hand up his leg, then under the leg of his shorts. Cam leaned back just enough that Rick could reach him anywhere he wanted. And when his fingers touched his balls, Cam cried out, his cock so sensitive that he nearly came with just his touch. "More. More, Rick, please?"

"Lean back. All the way." He did as he was told to do. His body hurt, he was so close to everything this man was giving him. "Christ, so much for getting to know each other a little first."

Rick's hand cupped his balls over his boxers. Cam had

almost decided to forgo his briefs in favor of taking a long shower after he was done here, but now he was so glad that he'd worn them. It would have been too much had he been able to touch him now — it would have been much too overwhelming.

As soon as Rick wrapped his hand around his cock, the punch to his body, the way that his body reacted, nearly had him coming straight up and off the seat he was on. It felt like he wasn't just on fire, but that he was covered in gasoline and a match had been flipped at him over and over.

"I need to taste you. I'm begging you to allow me to taste you." Rick was pulling at his shorts even before he could tell him yes or no. Not that he'd tell him to back off — his need was as difficult to control as Rick's seemed to be.

His shorts were in shreds by the time he was naked. His briefs hadn't fared much better. Cam watched Rick as he lowered his head to his cock. The anticipation of him touching him had Cam as hard as he'd ever been.

The moment that he touched him with his mouth, Cam came. His balls ached with the release, and he thought for sure that the top of his head had come off. As he lay there, breathing hard, Rick smiling at him, Cam took a moment to think about what had just happened.

"I didn't feel anything." Rick laughed, and Cam felt his face heat up. "That's not what I meant. I'm sorry. I meant that I didn't feel your emotions — I don't think."

"I'm sure you did. Just like I could feel yours — we were on the same thought process. I wanted you to come, and you did as well. I'm not a selfish lover. And with you, I will always want you to have more than I can take from you. But, I need you." Cam watched Rick, watched him stand up and hold his cock. It was dark with blood, tight with the need to come as hard as he had. And Cam had the overwhelming need to taste him. "Please, if you touch me with your mouth, I'm not going to be able to — Holy fuck, yes."

He tasted of heat. Never had he thought that he'd be able to taste such a thing, but he knew it as surely as he had him in his mouth. Rick was thicker than he was, his cock long too. The crown tasted of sex, and when he swirled his tongue around him, he got a small taste of his flavor, his cream. It was like he would have thought putting your tongue against an open electrical wire would feel. And he just couldn't get enough of it.

Cam had never done this before. He was taking his cues from the sounds that Rick made, the way that he held his head to him. And when he rocked into his mouth, filling him in a way that made his own cock hard again, Cam wrapped his hand around himself and fucked Rick with his mouth.

"I'm coming."

Nothing could have prepared him for the way Rick's cum filled his mouth and slipped down the back of his throat like it did. The incredible sensation of tasting someone. And when he came again, his cock spraying them both, Cam swallowed Rick's cock past the tightness of his throat and cried out when he was rewarded with more of the man. It was everything that he could have hoped for and more. Christ, he fell in love. Cam was in love with Rick Whitehall.

Rick staggered to the bench where he was sitting and just lay his head on his chest. Both of them were breathing hard — Cam could hear both their hearts as they seemed to be pounding out of their chests. When he wrapped his arm around Rick, never wanting this moment to end, it was his laughter, short and sort of exhausted sounding, that had him pulling the man up to look in his face.

"You've never done that before? Christ, I guess I'm glad for that. Any more experience with sex and I'd be dead about now."

Laughing, Cam felt better than he had since the accident. And when he laid back, Rick came with him, the two of them just enjoying the quiet of the moment after incredible sex.

"Two things I need to make you aware of. Nothing bad, but I'd like to have you know. My father is on his way to find me. He hasn't any idea where I am, but he's looking hard. And he isn't going to be happy that I've found you." Cam asked him why not. "Because he's been in this perfect state of denial since I told them I was gay. And — this is where it gets interesting — he's trying to blame my being gay for making him into what he is. A looser. Mom always said he was one before that. She hasn't any say in his life since she left him. She should have done so earlier, but she's doing all right now. She does hope that I never let him in my life again, which I will not do. She's the one that warned me before about him and his taking all the time."

"But neither of them know where you are, right?" He said that his mom did — she was the only person that he'd trust with that information — but yes, his dad didn't know. "I'm not sure that's a good idea. They could figure out that you're here and then get to her. I think, and this is just me, that we should ensure that she's all right. Perhaps hide her away better."

"You think?" Rick sat up. "You know, I never thought of that. She might just be the one that makes it so these other guys find you and your sister. And that would be really bad. I need to talk to…. Well, I should find me some clothing first. I don't want to be naked and have this conversation with Jake."

Cam reached out and touched his fingers to Rick's chest and thought of the clothing that he'd had on this morning. When it worked, Rick being dressed, he had to sit down. Rick asked him how he'd done that.

"I told you, I can do all kinds of things. And I'm not sure, but I would think, as my mate, you can do it too. Cattie can simply because she's my sister." Rick did the same to him, touching his hand to his chest. "I thought it would work with you too, and I'm glad that it does. There are all sorts of things that we'll share, I'm betting."

They both made their way to the stairs to find Jake and Forrest. Neither of them said anything about the magic that they now shared. What would be the point? They were mates, and he supposed that mates would share everything. Cam couldn't wait to see what else they shared. Life for the two of them was starting out well. He just didn't want the other shoe to drop. And it would—soon too, he'd bet. Nothing was ever perfect for very long.

~*~

Rick called his mom and the phone went to voicemail. It worried him a great deal. It wasn't like her to ignore a call from him, nor to be on the phone for very long. When he'd spoken to Jake and Forrest about her, they were in agreement with Cam that she needed to be somewhere safe, and with them was the best place to be.

"I don't know what's going on." Cam held his hand and said that they'd work it out. That he was going to see if he could reach her. "All right. But she's very sensitive about that sort of thing. I haven't any idea, but she might freak out a little if she doesn't know you."

"I'm really good at this. I've been able to do it for a long time. But I promise you, I'll be extra careful."

When Cam closed his eyes, Rick tried dialing her again and got the same results. Voicemail hadn't been set up on her phone. Rick knew why she didn't set it up—she didn't want his dad calling and leaving messages about needing money. But it didn't lessen his worry to know that—

"Rick." He didn't care for the sound of his name being said like that. He knew as surely as he was sitting there, something had happened. He begged him not to tell him just yet.

"Would you like something to drink? I'm thirsty. I think it was coming so hard." Rick was babbling, he knew that, but whatever information that Cam had for him, Rick did not want to know it. "I've been working on some things back at my house that I think—"

"Rick, have a seat." He felt his eyes fill with tears. He knew what he was going to tell him and shook his head. "I'm so sorry."

That was all he needed to say to him. Rick sat down hard on the chair he was nearest to and laid his head on the table. Someone had killed his mom. He didn't know who it was, or why they'd do such a thing to her, but she was gone. Rick realized that Cam was still talking when he lifted his head up.

"She is at the hospital now." He looked at him—hope was in his heart for a moment until Cam shook his head. "There isn't any way to save her now. She's been beaten too badly. But she's thinking of you as she fights with death. I'm going to contact Howard to see what he can to do save her."

"I should go to her." Cam shook his head again. "She's my mother. The only person in the world that believed in me."

"They're waiting on you to go to her. That's why they didn't kill her." Rick felt his belly rebel at the thought of his mother suffering for him. "She didn't tell them anything. And you should also know that it was your father that turned her over to them. He was paid a great deal of money to try and find you. I haven't any idea why they're looking for us through you, but that's what is happening."

"My dad? He actually told them to find Mom to.... Why

would he do something like that? She's never hurt anyone." Cam told him again that he was sorry. "I don't know what to do now. I don't understand any of this. What did finding me have to do with you and your sister?"

"Give me a moment and I can tell you."

Rick got up to pace. Just as he was pulling things from the refrigerator, Cattie came into the room. Rick had a feeling that she was there for him. He wasn't hungry, but the need to do something was overwhelming. And since he couldn't go to his mom, he'd feed the masses.

"I'm not ready." She nodded and asked if he was making sandwiches for all of them. "If you can, help. But don't talk about this yet, all right?"

"Yes, I'm fine with that."

They were putting the food on a platter when the rest of the household joined them. They were a large group, so Rick asked if they could use the dining room. More things were pulled from the cabinets—chips, pickles and anything else that looked like it might be good with turkey and ham sandwiches—when Jake said it was fine.

Rick looked around the silent group that he'd begun to think of as his best friends. He didn't have that many people in his life that he could lean on, but he did think he could have them here. Instead of playing with his meal any more than he had already, he shoved it away and began talking. Not what was on his mind, but what was in his heart.

"You all have come to mean a great deal to me. People that I wish my mom could have met. She was always there for me, telling me to keep my chin up, not to get down when people turned away from me when they heard about my sexual preferences. Also, she told me not to become a fat queer, because no one wants to see that." They all laughed. "I have no idea how my father knew that we were together, but because of him, your entire family might be hurt."

"We've been there before and have come out on top of it. This time was no different." Jake looked around the room, then back at him as he continued. "We're there for you as much as you'll be for us. We're the best kind of family, Rick — strong, nonhuman bastards that leave no one behind."

"Are you ready for some information?" Rick nodded at Cam, then shook his head. "I completely understand that. If you'd rather wait, that's all right with me. But I have to tell the others about some of the things I know now."

"Go ahead. If it's too much, then I'll leave. There isn't any reason for someone else to get hurt because of me." Rick reached out and was glad when Cam gave him his hand to hold. "First, is my mom gone?"

"No. But I'll get to that in a minute. Did you guys know that Howard was Quincey's maker?" No one knew, if the looks on their faces were any indication. "I didn't know that either until late last night. We were talking about what is going on here and Howard told me, like it wasn't any big deal. So, when we were in trouble, Howard called to Quincey to help him. That's the reason that Cattie and I were able to leave the store before it went up. Howard had enlisted the help of his child, Quincey."

"How does that fit in with all this?" Cattie smiled when Cam winked at her. "It's really too bad you've found your mate only to be dead by my hand in a couple of minutes. Bastard."

"But you love me," Cam spoke again. There was a large wipe off board in the room now, and it was just another thing that Rick wondered if he'd have too. "I'm writing this so that I can keep it all straight in my mind too."

He started writing all their names on the board. And when it didn't look like there was going to be enough room, it expanded to accommodate them. Cam was right, he was freakishly powerful.

"Okay, here we go. Quincey knew the two of you through Jenna. And Howard knew her. She called on his power too when it was needed. So, in turn, Cattie and I knew Jenna as well."

The lines on the board were twisted up, overlapping in a way that made Rick begin to understand why Cam had wanted it written down. It was overwhelming. As Cam continued, Rick thought of his mom. She was the sweetest person in the world. Never harming anyone, nor saying anything that would upset another. And now his father was going to pay for this shit. Rick was going to make sure he found out who had ordered whatever happened to her too.

"And that's why she's not there any longer." He looked at Cam when he realized he'd not been paying attention. He seemed to understand and repeated most of it again to him. "Quincey and Howard have been working as team, without telling us, to put us all together. One of them has taken your mother from the hospital and is currently working on saving her. It's not clear to me yet the extent of her injuries, but they're both trying to help her."

"Okay, we understand that part of the timeline. What about how Rick's dad knew where we were? I mean, what gave us away?" Cam said that they didn't know. "But I thought you said that he did — Rick's dad did."

"He *claimed* that he knew us through you, Forrest. Richard, Rick's father, believes that there are so few homosexuals that we all know each other. And figured that at some point in Rick's life, he's met us all. And if not him, then his wife for sure. The man is a real idiot." Cam sat back down as he continued. "So, in his lies, he told this man that, while he didn't know what we looked like, my sister and I, his wife would know. Going to see her was what they thought was going to be the end of this. But what they failed to figure on was the fact that she'd fight back, and that she was much stronger than she looked. Your mom managed to kill two of the men who came after her and injured the rest before she took a bullet in the chest. In answer to your question, she was picked up by Howard and Quincey to save her."

"Is she going to be all right?" Cam told Rick that he didn't know yet, but they were doing all they could to save her. "My father, he made a great deal of money from this, didn't he?"

"Yes, but only half of what they'd promised him. He was supposed to receive one million, but only half now and half when they caught up with my sister and I. You can imagine how pissed he is going to be when he doesn't collect on the other half." Rick put his hands down under the table. He didn't feel as if he deserved comfort just now. But Cam took his hand into his again. "Listen, it could be worse. If he knew that you were not only with me, but also my mate, he'd have someone looking harder than ever for us. Your mom, she more than likely saved all our lives."

"She would never have given you up. Or me, for that matter." Cam told him that he knew that about her. "This is just so crazy. Do you guys have any idea why these people are trying to find you? I mean, other than your freaky abilities, what did either of you do to have them so hyped up to get you?"

"I think I know." Henry cleared his throat before continuing. "They have a shipment coming in soon. Wally, my go to ghost, said that he's not sure what it is, but they want Cattie dead before it comes to fruition. They seem to think that she's so good at her job that killing her will leave them on easy street. And this might help, Wally said that she's messed up their plans before."

"That doesn't really narrow it down much." Henry told Cattie he was sorry. Wally wasn't all that good at things that were going on now. "No need to apologize. We have gotten a lot of information that we didn't have before. Does he know the man's name? The one that wants me gone?"

When Henry looked to his left and Rick turned to do the same, he didn't see anyone there, but he did believe that Henry did. And when he smiled, Rick knew for some reason, things might be working out for the better. At least this part of it would.

"He said that he didn't remember to catch that, but he's going to go there now. There were a great many pieces of paper on his desk, perhaps something there might help us out." Cattie nodded then put up her finger, as if she'd just thought of something. "He's not left yet if you're wanting something else."

"Does he have a daughter? And if so, what is her first name? There is a wife too, as well as a business partner, if my guess about who it might be is right." Wally left them, Henry said, and they retired to the living room. Cattie asked to be excused for a moment and left as well. She was a good cop and would know more than any of them about all this, Rick thought.

It was only just after two in the afternoon, and Rick felt as if he'd been running a marathon, gotten run over, and had been put to the side of the road for people to walk on. Christ, and after the best sex he'd ever had too. That was the only uplifting thing that he could think of right now.

Chapter 5

Wayne stood in the hospital room where the old broad had been. Christ, this was becoming an epidemic. People just up and disappearing like they were, and no one seemed to think anything was odd about that but him. This time, however, he knew that a vampire had done it. There had been just the slightest hesitation on the vamp's part that made him visible just long enough for Wayne to see him. The trouble now was he had to find someone that believed him about it, and for him not to say anything to the men working with him here. And now that he was sure what it was, he needed to figure out what they wanted to back the fuck out of his life.

"Sir, I've searched the entire floor, and there isn't any sign of Mrs. Whitehall. I even checked the floors above and below us." He nodded at Jamie, his right-hand man, and the biggest dumbass he'd ever known. "Do you suppose she might have left without being released?"

"No. I don't think she could have taken a breath without someone helping her. She had been messed up pretty badly." He'd been enjoying himself a little too much in trying to make her talk. She may or may not have known where the two of them were, but she didn't speak, didn't scream, or make even a small moaning sound when he was beating her to shit. "What have you found out about Mr. Whitehall, her spouse?"

"Gone. I do have someone tracking where he might have gone from here, but nothing so far."

Wayne had a feeling that they wouldn't find him, either. Giving him half a mil had been stupid. He'd told Dalton, and would again, how dumb he was for paying people off before they did any work for them. The man was forever taking the easiest route to get things done, and it was costing them time. They only had about seventy-two hours left before the shipment arrived.

Now Wayne had to make nice for his job, or people would be asking questions. And he hated questions that when he deemed it none of their business—which most of his personal life wasn't. It was no one's business but his own.

Wayne had always prided himself on being a good agent for the Feds. He'd done what was expected of him and nothing more. Even when an opportunity was opened up for him to take some cash or drugs, he didn't. But that was then, and the current Agent Leon wasn't such a goodie-two-shoes. And he had a great deal of wealth to show for it too.

Wayne took when he could, what he could, in any way that he could get by with it. He was the person that would come down hard on a crook, flashing his badge, and take whatever it was they had for himself. Several drug deals had been broken up by him, and he'd reaped every part of them as well. Selling it again to the—

"Sir, your phone is ringing." He'd been lost in thought, again. It worried him how much he'd be just standing there and not paying any attention. His mind was working overtime to figure shit out, and he was having trouble remembering even the smallest things, such as was he headed to the bathroom or finished? Shit like that would get him killed. Pulling out his phone, he answered it when he saw that it was his direct boss. It didn't even make him nervous any more when he called him.

"I've just gotten word that you're making rounds at the hospital, Agent. Are you now a doctor? Are you working out your rotation for tomorrow or something?" He never bothered answering him—Hal Cronkite was old and a pain in his ass. "Where are you right now, young man? You might remember, at least once in a while, that you do work for me."

"I remember that well, Agent Cronkite. I'm at the hospital now on the disappearance of a woman. I was here when the call came in and decided to lend a hand." He asked him how he'd ended up there. "My son, he broke his arm at school and they called me. You can ask the switchboard. I called them to explain why I'm not on call." The old fart would check, too. It was like him to check up on all his people, as he called those that worked for him.

Wayne had called the switchboard as soon as he got the call from Dalton that he was to go and see what he could find out from the elder Whitehall. Calling the switchboard to have the operator lie for him wasn't any big deal. It would cost him about ten grand, but he was off the hook from Cronkite for a few hours to pursue his own agenda.

Wayne had no children at all, no wife that he could sometimes use as an excuse for work, and his own mother had been dead for longer than he could remember. He would make sure not to use the same excuse twice, and to do that, he'd been keeping track of what he said on his phone's calendar. He didn't know what the fuck was up with the people he worked for. For an agency that prided itself on making sure that there were no lies in their department, they sure had screwed up with him.

Cronkite was still speaking as he made himself a mental note to make sure he catalogued this incident.

"Well, see that you make it in earlier tomorrow. I don't know if you're aware of this or not, but we're paid to get the bad guys off the street, not take our kids to the hospital for every little hurt or bruise." He pointed out that his arm had been broken. "So? Why didn't that wife of yours take care of it? I know that she's not working anymore. What was wrong with her taking care of your kid?"

"She's going to have a baby soon." That shut him up. For as much as Mr. Cronkite was a mean bastard, he loved that women still had children and that they reared them in the right way by not working away from home and hiring sitters—the wife doing that for her family, and especially for her man. His boss was as big a dork and sap as most of the men that he worked with, but that didn't lessen his hatred for him. "She's not any good at driving right now. I didn't want her to strain herself while she—"

"No, no. You did the right thing, taking your son so that she could rest. Yes, that was the only way to see it done. How are the rest of your children, Agent? I don't know as much about them as I do other families." Wayne wanted to laugh, then tell him that it was impossible to be very close to a figment of his imagination, the same for his other children. "You should bring them to the next shindig the company has. Introduce me to them. I'd like that."

"I'm sure they would as well. I speak of you so often, they more than likely think they know you as well as I do." They both laughed, but Wayne rolled his eyes. "The doctor is coming, sir. I must see what he has to say about the break. I'll speak to you later."

After checking the calendar to make sure that all was on there, he put the phone back in his pocket. Wayne had another look around to see what might have been left behind. Nothing. Not even a stray hair was found anyplace. After gathering what he could, he told the head nurse that they'd be back to them soon. On his way back home, he took the most indirect route just to be sure that no one was following him. Yeah, he was that paranoid, he thought to himself.

Getting home just after six, Wayne locked up his gun in the safe, took off his belt and put it in the closet, and decided that he was more comfortable in just his boxers and an old tee. Wayne decided that while he was on medical leave, granted to him by Cronkite for the next few days because of his wife and son, he'd get all the extra sleep he could. While he made his way to the kitchen to have leftovers again, he flipped on his recently purchased television to watch some news.

Wayne only watched the news in the evening to see if there was anything going on that he might have a hand in, and how close the police were to his crimes. They never were, so he had little to worry about. Usually the other people on there, the guys that had been arrested or killed, weren't anything like him in terms of being a bad guy. Wayne might give the illusion that he was simple-minded and backward, but that was because that was all he wanted a person to see. He knew beneath that little layer of skin he was as fucked up as the rest of the world. Perhaps more so than most.

When he was finished with his meal, he went to his office to make notes on his day. It was something that he'd been doing since he'd been in grade school making notes on his day to prove to anyone that asked that he was doing more than his fair share of housework, as well as gardening. His sister, Patricia, had always hounded him on that, telling their parents that not only hadn't he done a thing, but had spent most of his day in front of the television. It was then that he'd whip out his notes and show them, with times on the tasks, that he'd been much busier than even his parents had. Of course, they never saw it that way.

Patricia had been the golden child back then. He'd still get his ass beat or grounded for this or that, most of the time for things that she had done. What they didn't understand was that he didn't care for the things they took from him, and they gave him a reprieve from having to be normal. His getting into trouble would be because Patricia was a better liar than he'd been, and that she would talk the two older boys next door into doing her work if she let them touch her boobs. Since he didn't have anything those kids wanted to see, thank God, he'd been in trouble. Christ, she had been so easy.

Patricia had been killed a few years later. Not by the boys next door, as he always told her would kill her, but someone that she'd worked with at a fast food restaurant. She had wanted him to trade days off with her, and in exchange he'd be able to touch her. He hadn't settled for just a touch, but had taken her to the back room, where they were supposed to be cleaning up after closing time and torn her apart. Literally. He'd bet anything that they could still find parts of her in that fucking place if it opened again.

The manager had come into the store the next morning and found the man sitting on the floor with all of Patricia's body parts in neat, sliced up piles. Blood was on everything, from the ceiling to the floor, and even in the dining area. He had sliced her up on the slicer, going through bone, as well as muscle and skin, to present her on baking sheets to whoever came in — like he was going to make her into a raw Patricia sandwich for breakfast. It wasn't long after that that the restaurant had closed up and never opened again.

Once the news was over, Wayne made his way to the back porch and beyond. No one could see into his yard — he'd made sure of that by putting up a nine-foot-tall privacy fence. He had stuff back there that wasn't anyone's business. A safe haven, for starters.

When he went to the fallout shelter that had been put in his yard before he'd been born, no one could tell what he was up to. Opening the door to the shed then picking up the rug that was over the door in the floor, he was in lockdown in just minutes.

It wasn't out of date, like it had been when he'd first discovered it. Wayne had been updating things as he could, reading up on how to fix this or that on the Internet. And when that wasn't enough, he'd watch videos. There was so much free information out there that he didn't ever have to use any kind of repairman, nor have anyone coming to his home for anything. Wayne had managed to put in all new bulletproof windows to his house, as well as a new furnace to the shelter.

The rooms weren't all that large. Most of them weren't any bigger than a couple of bathroom stalls at the mall when he'd started down here. But he'd managed to figure out enough about expanding those as well, like for storage and being able to consolidate wherever he could. That made it so he had plenty of room to live down there, should it ever come to that. And he had food and water too.

The computer had been the most recent addition to his little home away from home. The Internet didn't want to work in the solid steel rooms. But when he'd been looking at videos for his own home on how to steal a connection from the neighbors, he saw one that showed how to pull it into the basement. His shelter was basically the same type of room, so he'd worked from there.

Opening the cam he had in Dalton's home, he saw that the servants were up to their usual laziness and figured that Dalton wasn't home. Wayne had set up Dalton's house in one afternoon so that he could spy on him. He had all the latest equipment—why not use it? he'd thought. The only room that he didn't watch, even though there was a camera in there too, was Debra's room. She was about as ugly and nasty as any woman he'd ever seen.

She wasn't plump, as Dalton called her—she was grossly overweight. He'd bet—and he'd never been very good at judging anyone's weight before…always guessed too low—that Debra weighted in at about four-fifty, easy. But she wore clothing that made her look like a sausage, all that fat in clothing that was better suited to someone about half her size. He avoided that room like the plague when he had to see what they were up to. Wayne had managed to catch Debra coming out of the bathroom once, nude, and he'd been sick for two days. Never again, he'd told himself.

Having all the equipment on him the day that he worked it out had made it very simple. Dalton had dismissed him—no other word for how he'd told him to leave. Wayne had just simply hidden in one of the other many rooms until the house was empty. There were servants, but they usually didn't leave the kitchen when the boss was away for the day, opting instead for watching the little television that was hidden away in the kitchen, just for them.

Wayne saw Debra come into the house with about two dozen bags not long before Dalton had gotten home. Some of them were brought up from the cab she'd come home in—the rest were dangling like pearl earrings for a fat sow from her arms. Running up the stairs, taking them as quickly as she could, had him thinking that Daddy didn't know she'd been shopping. But almost as soon as that thought had entered his head, he knew it to be wrong.

No one but Dalton had credit cards. He'd told him once that if you gave your family a card then you might as well give them an open account to all your worldly goods. Dalton would let them use his for the day, let them buy something pretty, or even purchase an outfit for an upcoming event where he wanted them to be there for him. But they'd have to return the card as soon as they returned. With, of course, all the receipts.

Wayne did something that he'd not done since he'd first looked into her room—he turned the cameras on in Debra's room. The bags were just as he'd thought they'd be, lying all over the bed and floor like a carpet made from the different colored bags. When she dumped one of them on the bed, he could see that they were panties and bra sets. Knowing that he didn't want to see her trying one of them on, he flipped the camera to the left of the bathroom doorway and looked around for some clue as to why her mother had come up missing.

Wayne had already figured out that she'd been murdered. When someone disappeared like she had, that was the only thing it could be. Another person that had come up missing was Dalton's previous partner, Benny. He was positive that Benny and Dalton's wife had not been banging each other. First of all, Benny had to have been about sixty. And Dalton's wife looked like a horse with its head on its ass, and it brayed like a jackass.

The daughter had gotten her looks from her mother. She looked just like her, and even had that annoying laugh that made him want to pull out a gun and blow her tongue out of her mouth. Debra had probably put on about forty pounds in the last few months. Wayne knew for a fact that Dalton had paid for her to go to some gym to slim up. The only slimming that she could do was to have someone cut her hands off so she'd not be able to shove things into her pie hole. Her mother had been only slightly lighter, at a daunting four hundred.

There was a note of some sort on the vanity in Debra's room. Zooming in on it as closely as he could, he could see that it was a note from her mother. Trying to read it was nearly impossible, but there were a few words on it that he could make out. *Left*, *time away*, and *I'll be back*.

Wayne wondered aloud if Dalton had made his wife write the note, or if she'd really just left and would return. It was a longshot if the note actually said that, but he didn't care much. He'd get in there and find out sometime over the next three or four days. It was important for his level of trust with Dalton to know everything. And he would before too much longer.

~*~

Cam woke up in the big bed alone. He knew that Rick had to get up a lot during the night. He had some muscle damage from gunshot wounds, like Cam did, that would tighten up if he was too still for too long. And since he'd broken his shoulder playing football in college, he had trouble with that as well. Rick didn't take pain pills unless it was really bad, he'd told Cam. And last night he'd taken two of them.

"The sex." Cam told him he was sorry about that. "I'm not. Christ, it feels too good for me to be stopping because I hurt afterwards. You have given me that. I don't know what I'd do now if you weren't here."

"You might not be so sore." Rick told him that it was well worth it. "I hope you'll say no, or just go to bed when you hurt this much again."

"I'll try. That's the best I can do for you." After smiling and kissing him quickly on the mouth, Rick laid down. "Now, be a good nurse and come wrap around me. The warmth really does

70

help a great deal." It must have helped, along with the pain pills, because he was asleep before Cam was.

After finishing his shower and getting dressed, Cam made his way downstairs. He found Cattie in the dining room holding little Jenna while she ate. Mostly Jenna was doing the eating— Cattie was just staring at her. When she saw him, she handed the baby to him and started in on her own food. He asked her why she had her if she didn't want her.

"I do want her. A great deal. The reason that I've not eaten is because she's so beautiful, and I can't keep myself from just wanting to stare at her, in the event she does something I might miss." Cam told her she was nuts. "I know that. Christ, she's a beauty, isn't she?"

"She is at that." Walton joined them a few minutes later and asked Cam if he wanted anything to eat. "I don't want to cause any trouble."

"No trouble, sir. We are enjoying everyone being here as much as Lord Jake and Lord Forrest are. And we're trying new things as well. Cook has made blueberry pancakes and has been able to make a Monte Cristo as well." Cam asked what they had made for his sister. "She had eggs, toast, and bacon. Would you like that, sir?"

He sounded so sad about the possibility of him having the same as Cattie had. It was a good, solid meal, but he'd bet that when offered something more, Cattie had declined. She wasn't really keen on breakfast for breakfast anyway. She liked that meal for dinner. That way her belly, she claimed, was more up for it.

"Actually, I'd love some blueberry waffles, if you have the resources to make them. I don't want to put anyone out."

Walton assured him that he wasn't and went to the kitchen. A few moments later, he'd brought Cam not only juice but a cup of hot tea, as well as a fresh bottle for Jenna. He was still feeding her when Rick came in to join them.

After a quick kiss to him, Rick stole a piece of Cattie's bacon and sat down opposite him. He watched the baby while she ate her own food, without saying anything. Cam had noticed that about him—he was a thinker, and rarely said much until he got his plans, or whatever, all laid out in a good order.

"This thing with my parents—I was wondering if you could find out something for me. I would need you to pick my dad's head for it. Not that I care if you harm him or not, but I have an idea how to use him to keep us safer for a bit longer." Cam's plate was set in front of him as the baby was handed off to Rick. Walton asked him what he wanted to eat. "The same as Cam, please. But can I have ham instead of sausage? I don't care for bacon either."

When Walton left with another order, Cam dug into his breakfast while the other man explained. He wanted him to find out if he could see the faces of the men that he'd hurt Mom over. Cam asked if he might know them.

"No, but you might. I mean, you have access to all the most wanted, right? I know you've not been to work in a little while, but you'd remember their faces if they had been on the list before you'd left, right?" He said that was a wonderful idea. "I have them on occasion. But that could help us narrow some more of this down. If we have names, it will make things easier to find."

"I can do that."

When he tucked into his breakfast again, he reached out for Rick's father. The man was so stupid, spending the money on everything from hookers to fast cars. At the rate he was going, Cam figured that he'd be broke again by the end of the week— and today was Thursday. Digging a little deeper into his mind, he saw his greed and his thoughts of selling out his wife more often. It had been a nice payday for him, even at the cost of her almost dying.

Cam would tell Rick that later, what sort of father he had, but he'd bet he knew that already. When he found the thread to the men, Cam searched his memories for the faces of them. As soon as he saw the first man, Cam felt like he was going to be sick. The second man, both men he knew, had him leaping up from his chair and running to the bathroom that was close to them.

Cam threw up everything on his belly. Not looking at what he was spewing, Cam knew that it would be a while before he was able to eat waffles of any kind again. Sitting on the floor, the tile wall behind him, Cam thought of what he'd just found out. No one was going to forgive him for this. Christ, he didn't know if he could forgive himself.

The knock at the door was from his sister, and he told her he was fine, that he'd be out in a minute.

He didn't want to though. There wasn't any way that he thought that he could face them after this. Cam was being hunted by the only man in his division that he'd ever trusted — his own boss. The man that he'd poured out his whole life to one night was gunning for not just him, but Cattie as well. Cam was glad now that he'd never mentioned what he could do to anyone from his job. Christ, that would have been a shithole of a mess had he done that.

Standing up, he washed his face, then rinsed his mouth to get rid of the nastiness that he'd just thrown up. Looking at himself in the mirror, he just knew that he was going to be asked to leave, and Cattie would follow and get hurt. So would Rick, but the man could probably take care of himself better than his sister.

Opening the door, he was surprised to see who he thought was Wally there. The ghost, as far as he knew, wasn't visible to anyone but Henry and Paddy. Paddy's sister Christy, he thought, could see him too, but not Cam. When he nodded to the elderly man, he smiled at him.

"I'm Wally, as you might have guessed. The magic that comes from you, we're assuming that it's the reason that everyone within the household can see me now. I so much...I'm sorry. My lord sent me to find you, sir. He wanted me to tell you that his mother is on the mend. But she has been converted to save her life. He thought that it would be better coming from you to tell Rick about her." Cam nodded and said that he'd take care of it. "Good. Something else. You should give people a chance before you decide that you're going to be kicked out of house and home. These are the best kind of people you could have around you. Whether it's good stuff or bad, they'll be right there with you."

"Thank you. I wasn't aware that you could read minds." Wally said that he couldn't, but he knew what he'd seen in his thoughts. "Then how did you see that if not reading my mind?"

"I don't remember what they called it, but you're shouting out what you saw by being sick about it. Since I knew that nobody here would hurt you, it had to be somebody that you worked with. When I overheard them talking about what you'd done for your mate...well, let's just say that I can add up stuff better than most can." Wally's grin was as big as his head, and then some. "Numbers ain't my strong suit, mind you, but I can see when things are ticking away. I'm going to learn how to read soon too, if I can find me somebody to help me."

"Christy." Wally asked him what he meant. "Christy can read, and teach you better than most, I'm betting. You should ask her. I'm willing to bet that she'd have as much fun teaching you as you did showing her how to play chess. She told me that you taught her."

"I never thought of that. I'm gonna talk to her after you all have dinner. Thank you, sir. And remember what I told you—you can't be in a better family than this one. See if I'm not right." Cam promised him that he'd do it. "Thank you for telling your mate about his momma. She'll be fine, but Lord Quincey doesn't want him to be upset when he finds out. They can work on that now, before she can come here."

"I will."

Wally disappeared, and Cam laughed. The man was a wonder, but he liked him. Heading to the dining room, he knew this was going to be hard on all of them, so he chickened out and told Rick about his mom first.

"She's all right then?" Cam said again that she was now a vampire. "I don't care if she's a stalk of grass in the yard, so long as I know that she's safe and all right. When did they say that she'd be here? Or should I wait before pestering someone?"

"I'd wait. She will be recuperating for a few more days, Wally said, but she's all right otherwise." Cam looked up and down the table. Since he'd left, the rest of them had joined them for breakfast. It was time. "I know the people that are looking for us. I mean, I know them from working with them. I'm so sorry that I didn't see it earlier. My boss, Wayne Leon, and his underagent, Jim Tosca, are working on a project with Dalton Carter."

"I know Dalton Carter." Cam nodded at his sister. "I should have known that fuck turd was in on this. I should have. Christ, this isn't going to be any easier than before, except that we know their names now."

When she got up to pace, no one commented on it. But there was more to tell, and Cam started to explain what he knew.

Most of it was supposition, but there were enough facts that he should have guessed about him before today. When asked, he reached out to the other man's mind and carefully extracted what he needed.

"Tosca doesn't know as much as the other two. He's only been working with the two of them since I was put on medical leave. But he's in deep enough that we need to worry about him. His job is to watch the other people in the two departments that they head, and make sure that no one is talking about anything that they're in on." Cam laughed a little. "He's using a watch recorder that kids wear to document everything. But he does download it onto his computer at night. I can fuck that up from here. So, after I get into the computer and take the information, I can have the information relayed to here."

With this much information, one would think this would be a walk in the park. But it was more like walking in a tar pit, and all you had to hold onto was a gallon of more tar so that you'd not get caught. He didn't want anyone to get hurt, and he was sure that they would. And he might end up dead before that happened too. It would figure. He'd found someone to love, and it would be taken from him too soon.

It was all he could do to not look at Rick. He had his good news about his mom—perhaps he'd not think about Cam's involvement in the rest. But he knew that was a pipedream, and that the man would think of nothing else. Cam would deserve anything that he got. And he'd take it like a man too. He loved Rick very much and was deeply depressed that things were about to fall apart for both of them. Leaning back in his chair, he let the rest of them talk around him. Cam needed to figure out a plan where he could hide out until this was finished. He knew that the people of this house would throw him to a pack of wolves as soon as one could be gathered up.

Chapter 6

"Let me get this straight. You're packing your bags before you talk to Jake and Forrest—without talking to me, let me remind you—because you're sure that they're going to kick you out of the house and my life. You do know that is the stupidest thing that you could have ever thought, don't you?" Cam asked him why. "Because, moron, you go, I go. But that just isn't going to be the case. We're here because these men need us as much as we need them. And they're not in the habit of throwing people out because a former boss is a fucking crook."

Rick waited for Cam to say something, anything. But all he did was sit on the bed, his face wearing the look of defeat. He didn't want to see that. He wanted to see him happy. They had each other, they had names to help them, and had enough magic to make sure that the criminals were all in the shit tank when this went shit up.

"I don't want you hurt." Rick sat down next to him on the bed, shoving the duffle to the floor. "Those are clean clothes—you know that, don't you?"

"I don't care. If it means that you're going to finally listen to me, then I'll piss on them if that's what is needed." Cam smiled. "Good. And so you know, I've been talking to Forrest. He said that if you even dare to leave this house to keep them out of this, he'll shift and tear into your ass. I think he means that."

They were both laughing now, and Rick could have jumped for joy. He didn't want to leave here. He thought, like the others did, that this was the best place for them to be for this. No one knew where they were, and they had the backing of some heavy hitters — tigers, bears, wolves, and vampires — plus, the magic that seemed to be all around them. There couldn't be any better odds than that. He told Cam what he'd been thinking.

"These men, they play for keeps — you understand that, don't you? I mean, they wanted myself and my sister dead. Mostly her." He thought about what else he'd seen in the mind of Tosca. "He'll be there tomorrow night, and Tosca will be there monitoring the shipment as it comes in."

"What is it coming in, do you know?" He said that Tosca didn't, so he didn't, but he could look at Carter if he wanted. "Not yet. If it's bad, we should all be together, so we can figure this out as a group."

Rick got up when Cam did. The two of them were still on tender ground, and the worst part was that all this shit with these men wasn't helping them. Thinking of all the things they could be doing right now — not just sexually, but in general — instead of waiting for this to be taken care of boggled the mind. But they would, and they'd have a good life together.

Cam headed to the living room when Forrest called them in after they went downstairs. Rick hoped for now that he'd convinced Cam that he couldn't leave, and that whatever Forrest and Jake thought of things, they'd reassure him that they weren't going to do anything but help them.

As soon as they entered the room, Cam stopped. Everyone,

including the vampires, was there waiting on them.

"We've brought your mom home, Rick. Cattie is with her now, showing her around the new place where she's staying. I'm sorry, but there wasn't any other way to—" Rick hugged Howard to him, tightly, and his emotion was felt by everyone there. "I take it you're not unhappy about this."

"No. She's well, and that's all that matters to me. I'm sure that she told you the same thing." Howard nodded, and Rick could see the relief on the vampire's face. "All right then. Cam and I have more information. And I think a plan. But it will take all of us. And when I say all of us, I do mean that. Even Wally."

The man appeared in the room, and Rick wondered at that because he could see him. Rick started to comment on that when Cattie came into the room with his mom. Christ, she was beautiful—they both were, just in different ways. His mom looked like she was glowing now, her happiness all over her body. So was Cattie, which made him worry about other men when this was over. He was going to talk to Cam about it as soon as this crap was finished.

"Some of you know her already, but I'd like for you all to meet Rick's mom. She's the best there is, and I won't hear an argument out of any of you on this. She told me that I was pretty, and that makes her perfect in my handbook." Mrs. Whitehall—Patsy, she asked to be called—said that she was a little prejudiced. "Yes, I am. You've been through hell and back, and I'm so happy to see you that I could just cry."

She did. Cattie wasn't normally emotional, Rick would bet, but his mother really had gone through a great deal. Cam hugged Patsy too, then said that they should all get down to business.

"I want that bastard dead. I'd like to say that I'll do it, but I'm not so sure that I can. After forty years of marriage, he goes and hurts me and others. I wish I could tear him apart right this minute." Her fangs showed then, and she was embarrassed. Going to Howard, she leaned against him and he put his arm around her and held her. He, along with Quincey, to a lesser degree, was her maker. "I'm sorry. I'm still getting used to all this."

"As I told you upstairs, Patsy, you're here, and that's all we care about." Everyone in the room nodded. It was nice to have her there. He knew that both he and Cam would be much more relaxed now.

"Tosca, James Tosca, is a part of what is going on. He'd nothing more than a snitch. While I was coming down here, I had him work on his computer so that we could clone it. He won't remember doing it, and he'll never see what we're doing, even if he's online. But there is a shipment coming in tomorrow night. While he doesn't know what's on it, he's very excited to be able to be a part of it. Point man, he thinks he is." Jake asked Cam if anyone might know what was coming in. "I can get into their heads from here. Both of them are making plans, but I've not looked yet. I wanted to make sure that you all understand that this is going to just be a pinch. In my opinion, we should only take this shipment, and have the police involved or something like that to make them realize that we—Cattie and I—are on to them. It'll piss them off, and a pissed off crook is a stupid one. Or in this case, stupider."

"I agree. When one of my clients from where I worked before would lose their cool, they'd do and say things that would land them right back where they'd started. One of the reasons that I left." Jake smiled at them, clearly embarrassed. "Not the only reason, but that was the start. Tell us the plan. And so you know, I'd go with the Feds. I know a couple of them from working with them before. They're out of the D.C. office."

"I like that." Rick asked if he would get in touch with them when they were finished here. "We'll work on a plan, tell them what we have, then go from there. You think that'll be all right with them?"

Jake said it would. Everyone looked at Cam when he laughed.

"You're not going to believe this. The shipment coming in is cigarettes, then it's headed to Mexico. And the shipment isn't at all a *ship*ment — it's a couple of trucks coming in. And since they took them across three state lines to get this far and will do more when they head to the finish line, we're going to have fun with this one." Cattie laughed too, then Jake and Forrest. Rick asked what was so funny. "There are very strict laws concerning how many and how much of that sort of stuff you can take into Mexico. You can only take two cartons of them, or fifty cigars. There are weight limits on things like tobacco and wine too. But they're very pissy about it if you bring in more. Like long prison terms in Mexico's system."

"So, once they leave wherever they are here, we'll get them for attempted contraband, as well as crossing the state lines. That, too, is a biggy in the States." Forrest looked at Cam again as he continued. Rick understood, but he was still a bit slow on why that was funny. "Are the cigarettes stamped? God, I hope not. That is going to really toast this guy. And you can bet he'll be willing to squeal on the other two for a little time off." Cam was shaking his head at Forrest even as he asked the question.

Rick still wasn't sure what all was going to happen. He knew his place in the plan, what he was to do. But when it came to the arrests and the humor around that, he was still a little behind. Not that it mattered much. The number of good laughs about this was contagious, and he was soon laughing with them. Cam said that he'd explain it to him if he wanted, but

Rick declined. Explaining it to him might make him understand more, but in the end, it didn't really matter if he was up on the laws governing tobacco.

The call that was made to D.C. resulted in the plan being okayed by the Feds. They had to tell their boss, the president, on this, but he would be all right with it as well, they were told. One less scumbag on the streets was what they all thought.

But Rick still wasn't comfortable about this. Someone, he knew was going to get hurt. When Cam was alone, Rick went to speak to him. It was his plan, after all, and he wanted at least a little assurance.

"How will this affect Carter and Leon? I mean, I understand that this Tosca person will more than likely tell on them. But what if he doesn't?" Cam said that they had enough on him to put him away for the rest of his life. And he was positive that he'd take a deal. "Okay, you're very sure about this, so I can't help but be sure too. But I'm also worried what kind of stupid shit these men will do to get back at you."

"I'm not so worried about them getting back at us as I am them getting off for some reason." Cam and he were the only two people left in the living room. The others had gone to get some other work done. "I do worry about you too. I know this kind of crap and what to expect, but you don't. I don't want anything to happen to anyone that I love."

"You love me?" Cam nodded and said that he did. "I'm in love with you as well. I knew that it would come over us fast, but I just didn't expect it to be so much. You know, almost overwhelming to me."

"It is for me as well. Oh, before I forget to tell you, you're an immortal. I guess we all are. We got that from being considered a part of Jake and Forrest's family. Quincey told your mom a bit ago, and I overheard them." Rick wasn't sure what to say so he didn't say anything. It was exciting to know that he'd be around with him for a long time. Immortality wasn't anything he'd ever thought of before, and he was thrilled to death that he'd found Cam to spend it with. "Henry said that you're going to help him and Paddy with their book. I'm so glad to hear that. I'm sure that you can give them some help on it that they might not have thought of."

"I'm just hoping that no one finds out about me working with them. I don't want any of this to come down to hurt them either." Cam already knew about Rick's book and what had happened with that. "To be honest with you, I was thinking of writing again myself. I'll have to find something to do when you're out saving the world."

"Not so much the world as just the little bit of it you and I are on." They both laughed. "I've been thinking about houses. Do you have one?"

"No. I never saw the reason to put down permanent roots before. Now, with you, I would love to be able to have a place to call our own. And I would love for Cattie and my mom to live with us."

"Great. Did you know that your mom has claimed me as her own kid? She said that she's very happy for us, but happier still that we're all here together. I have a house—so does my sister. Hers is smaller because it's the house my parents started out in. Not that it's tiny, but its smaller than the one I own. I've not lived in it for years, not since I was starting out. But this morning I called my staff and asked them to go get things opened up and cleaned. They're excited to meet you as well." Rick was suddenly intimidated. "Don't. Don't do that."

"You have money." Cam said that they had money. "I have some too—enough to pay my taxes for the year and perhaps have a burger out. I had a great deal at one time, but the blood sucking attorneys—I had to say that—they took a great deal of my cash to represent me and win. My father thinks I'm rich—that's what keeps him coming around. He thinks I'll give it to him. But I barely have two grand."

"With this thing I can do, I have been able to turn mine and my sister's money into a great deal. If neither of us wanted to work again, we'd not have to. While I have more than her, it's not mind-blowingly different. We're billionaires several times over. I think that Jake and Forrest are just above us on the richest couple charts."

~*~

Dalton watched the big trucks on his computer. The little tracker that they'd insisted on having on the loads was fun. He could see each of their stops, when they turned onto a road, as well as when they put fuel into the big sucker. And even how much they put in. This was the most fun he'd had in a while. Then Debra walked into his office again.

Christ, she was as bad as her mother had been about whining. He wanted to enjoy himself a bit longer, but no—she had to come in and take away from his fun. Dalton asked her, as calmly as he could, what was wrong now.

"I'm fat. Why didn't you tell me that I was getting fat?" That was a loaded question if he ever heard one. "I need to get rid of all this or I'm going to die. The doctor this morning said that I was grossly overweight, and that I have diabetes too. I don't want to have that. I don't understand how he came to that, Daddy. I don't eat that much sweets."

Lies, he wanted to tell her. "Honey, how can you say that? You love sweets." He was trying to tread carefully here. "Just the other morning you were telling me how you'd eaten an entire apple pie that was meant for dinner. And you even had a gallon of ice cream with it. You told me that yourself."

"Why didn't you tell me that was fattening? This is all your fault, Daddy. You hired those people in the kitchen to be such wonderful cooks, and I got fat because of you." He was itching to do the same to her as he had to her mother. "I want you to fix this. Now. I can't stand being made to be a diabetic."

"My fault? How the hell did you come to that?" He took a deep breath when her lower lip began to quiver. Christ, he hated to see that, and her bawling now meant that he'd never get back to his fun. And the trucks were due tonight. "Look, honey. I'll have a talk with the doctor. Perhaps he's made a mistake. And once I talk to him, then he'll work—"

"I want you to kill him." Dalton didn't move, not even to reach for his gun when she pulled out one and pointed it at his chest. "If you don't kill him, then I will. And I want his offices burned down. He has it on my record that I'm fat and sick. If you don't kill him today, I'm going to kill you right where you're sitting."

This was a Debra that he'd never encountered before. He was both proud of her and terrified. She seemed to be very calm about pulling a gun on him, and Dalton was going to kill her for it. Too bad, really. She might have fit well in his little ventures.

Wayne came in the room then and pulled out his own gun and shot her in the head. When she was falling forward, her body making a thud that could have been heard for miles, he shot her twice more, and it was all Dalton could do not to piss his pants when Wayne turned the gun on him.

"You gonna reach for that gun of yours?" Dalton asked him why he'd do that. "I just shot your daughter. I don't expect that to go over too well."

Neither of them moved. It wasn't until Dalton leaned back in his chair that he let out the breath he'd been holding. Shaking his head at the other man, he was relieved when he finally put his own gun away.

"She was going to kill her doctor for saying that she was fat." Dalton didn't expect any comment from Wayne and was startled when he laughed. Then the humor of the situation hit him. "I guess she'll lose that nasty weight now, won't she? And she will be the first person in the history of the world, I'm betting, who cured her diabetes in one afternoon. Christ, I thought for sure I was a fucking dead man."

"You have no idea how startled I was when I heard her talking. I didn't catch the part about the doc, but she said that she was going to kill you, and that sort of made me pissy with her." They both laughed again. "Now what do we do with her? You know as well as I that she's not going to be an easy clean up. You'll be lucky if they don't charge you triple for this."

He didn't care. Christ, they could charge him five times as much. Just having her gone would make things so much easier and better for him. Dalton had known, from the moment he said I do to her mother, that she, and later their daughter, would try and drain him dry. And he was right. Picking up the phone, he opened his computer again to see that the trucks had stopped just as they had crossed over into Ohio.

After making arrangements to have his dry cleaning done again, he and Wayne moved out of his office and moved to the study, taking his computer with him. Telling Wayne about what he was watching, he was dismayed that the trucks were still paused at the state line.

"I wonder what could be keeping them there for so long. You don't think they've run into trouble, do you?" Wayne said that he'd check with his office. Perhaps someone there knew what was going on. While he was on the phone, Dalton thought about Debra.

She'd actually pointed a gun at him. Did she think that

there'd be no consequences for that? Christ, what was this world coming to when a woman could just go into a man's office and make demands like that on the one that kept them safe? He looked at Wayne when he got off the phone.

"Nothing. I was thinking perhaps they might be getting gasoline. You know that the prices are cheaper here than they are some places?" No, Dalton didn't know that, but he didn't drive, so that wouldn't have meant anything to him anyway. "I'm betting that they're getting them something to eat and gassing up. You know, gas and go sort of thing."

"I suppose. What have you found out about Whitehall? That fucker has our money, and he's out there running around like we got what we paid him for." This time Wayne didn't bring up paying for information before you got it. "I don't suppose you had any luck finding him, did you?"

"No. The little shit is out there, as you said. And he could be telling anyone who we are." Dalton pointed out again that they'd not used their real names. "Do you think perhaps we should have changed our faces too? Do you have any idea how easy it would be for him to say, hey, that's them? Those two that have their pictures on the wall there. Fucking little shit. When I find him, and I will, I'm going to make him rue the day that he skipped out on us."

Dalton was sure that either one of them would have done the same thing. They'd have been better at doing it, but they'd have skipped town too. Dalton asked Wayne about the woman, the man's wife. He was shaking his head even before he answered him.

"Still unaccounted for. I still think some vampire found himself a good meal, and she's as dead as Debra is. But I need to know one hundred percent that's what happened." Dalton agreed with him. "I wish now that I'd let someone else try and get the information from her. I'd feel a good deal better knowing that she couldn't ID us either."

"Yes, well, we've both made some pretty big mistakes. Nothing that money can't fix, but we need to get her and that fucking husband of hers."

The doorbell rang, and he went to get it. Waving Thomas, his only staff, off, he told him it was for him. Opening the door to the dry cleaners, he was surprised. But when he saw the cleaner, a man that he knew well, he relaxed. Handing over the cash, he went back to the room where Wayne was.

"I have something else that needs to be taken care of if you're up to it." Wayne said that was what partners were for, and for some reason that struck Dalton oddly. He paused in his footsteps when he realized what Wayne was doing—he was looking at his computer.

"The trucks have started to move now."

Going to his computer, he made a point of taking it from the other man. This was his, and Wayne had better learn who was in charge. When he repeated what he'd said, commenting on the trucks beginning to move, Wayne wisely said good. After that, Dalton couldn't get him out of his home fast enough.

There was something going on. Dalton didn't know what it was, but he was not comforted by having Wayne in his corner any longer. He thought again about him having his gun pointed at him, and he shivered. Yes, Dalton thought, there was most assuredly something going on, and he'd get to the bottom of it. And soon.

Chapter 7

Cam looked over the paperwork while the four men were down on their knees in front of him. He knew that they'd had no idea that they were transporting contraband, but that made them no less guilty. They're supposed to check the cargo in their trucks before they even left the place where they picked their cargo up. He looked at them again—agents, friends of Jake's, were standing behind each man. Cam was almost too excited to speak. Not only had they given up everyone's name, but they'd also said where they had come from and where they were headed after making a stopover in Ohio. Heading to Mexico with their cargo was going to mean a long prison stay for everyone involved. And they'd pointed out where both the trackers were on their loads too. It was almost too good to be happening.

Cattie came around the side of the truck. She and another agent were going over the locks that sealed up each of the trucks. Nothing matched, she told him. That, too, should have been checked by the drivers. This was getting worse with everything they ticked off. Cam looked at the men just as Cattie spoke.

89

"It's all here." She handed him the paperwork that had been in each of the trucks—their true driving sheets, not the ones that they would show to a cop if pulled over. "They've been driving for the last sixteen hours. I'd say that would be okay, considering that they're double teaming it. But none of the other men in each has a license, much less one that has a rider for them to be able to drive a rig. So, they're about eight plus hours off the mark for that as well."

She was having fun, and it showed in every move she made. Cam had to refrain from hugging her every time something else came up in their favor. This was such a big deal that they were going to be all right after this ordeal was over. At least he hoped so.

"Agent Henderson?" He'd not been called that for a while now, and it took Cattie nudging him to make him remember. "Were you aware that there is a report, sir, that you're dead? And so is your sister? None of us are going to say anything— we know where this is headed—but when this is done, my boss would like to see you both. He said that it's important that he knows what you know."

"That's fine. We have to finish this now, as you're aware. The drivers that you have on the trucks, they know what they're to do once they reach their destination? I don't want any mess ups this late in the game." The agent—ATF...Cam thought his name was Carmichael—said that they'd been rehearsed as to their duty when they got to where the paperwork said to go in Ohio. "And the rest of the group of men you brought, they know not to show themselves until we say so?"

"Yes, sir." The man smiled. "They're all so excited to get this taken care of they're terrified of messing up. We've been working on this for a while now, trying to figure out where the tobacco had been coming from and how it got to the border. I made sure that I had the best on those trucks, and the very best at the other end. They're just waiting for word from you to go in and take care of this for us all. The chopper, it'll be here in about two ticks. If you're ready, we can get going as soon as it lands."

He nodded. Cam was getting full cooperation from everyone on this. It wasn't every day that you got to take down not only an FBI deputy director, but an associate deputy director too. Carter and Leon were top dogs in their offices, and Cam was going to take them both down with the help of fellow agents.

As soon as the chopper landed, they were running toward it when a man hopped off. Not really paying any attention to the stranger — Cam was more concerned about keeping his head — he nearly ran the president down in his haste to get going.

"Sir, I didn't — I don't think we expected you on this trip." He looked at Carmichael and he was grinning. "All right, it looks as if I was the only one that didn't expect you on this trip. I'm sorry I wasn't better prepared to meet you."

"You're doing just fine, Henderson. Come on, let's get going, and you can tell me about your plan as we go. I have to tell you, Henderson, this is quite a coup for you and your sister, and for the ATF too. The Department of Alcohol, Tobacco and Firearms is taking a second seat to the two of you. Caitlynn, she's damned good too, from what I've been hearing from my men." His sister was going to have a brick. And he wasn't going to tell her who he was riding with. "When this is finished, I'd like to sit down with the two of you and your men to see how you came up with this. I'm sure that you won't take all the credit, but I'm to understand that you and Caitlynn have been working together all along on this."

"Yes, sir. Some others and I have been involved from the start." He nodded at him. "You know Jake Winslow and Forrest

Stout? They've been more than a little helpful. Without them, Henry Myers, and Patrick Garrett, I don't think it would have been as smooth as it has been thus far."

"Yes, so I heard. Jake, his grandmother was a very close and personal friend of mine for a lot of years. Too bad that her son was such a nightmare. I'm sorry about that. I'm to understand that he's been sentenced and is going to be spending the next two hundred years or so in lock down." That's what Cam had heard too, but not from Jake. He'd heard it from Forrest, who had been keeping things low-key for Jake since the day it had been announced. "What are we going to do as soon as we get there?"

He told him the entire plan, and who had come up with the different parts of it. None of them were leaving anything to chance. Carter and Leon were going to meet the trucks at an abandoned airstrip in six hours. The agents were already in place. After that, the two of them, as well as Tosca, would be arrested, and anyone else involved with them.

Tosca had been well informed for someone that hadn't had a big role in all this. He'd known dates, where the meeting place was. The names of all those involved. They didn't even have to offer him up any sort of deal. Almost as soon as he was taken into custody, he started talking like he had pent it all up for a while and had just been waiting to start spewing. He also gave up his little recording device but asked for it back when they were done—he said that he'd paid ten bucks for it. Cam thought perhaps the man thought that he wasn't going to prison at all, but that wasn't the case, not as involved as he was, making him just as guilty as the drivers had been.

Getting out of the chopper about forty minutes later, Cam and President Wendell met with his sister, as well as Rick. Jake had known, and so had the other three. Cattie looked like she might be willing to murder him, but later. It was still a few hours before the trucks were to arrive, and they waited for Carter and Leon to show up. According to Tosca, they were supposed to be here at six-thirty, so that there would be time to have a nice dinner afterwards to celebrate.

"Are you ready for this?" He nodded at Rick, who had been standing on the sidelines since they arrived. Cam asked him why he was doing that—he kept walking away like he was in the way. "That's the president. I don't want him to get the wrong idea about you and I."

Cam laughed and pulled him in for a kiss. "I don't care what sort of idea he gets about us. But I do want him to have the right one—that you and I are a couple. Until death us do part. All right?" Rick threw back his head and laughed. "All right then. Now, I hate to have you do this, but you will stand back with him, won't you? I know that you and I are immortal, but I still don't want you hurting anymore. Not because of this."

"I don't want to be hurt either. And I have a list of houses that we can go look at if you're still thinking about selling your own." Cam told him he wasn't sure. "I'm not either, but until we have time to go over your home, I've decided not to call anyone to help us. I don't know why you're so worried about it. I'm sure that it's a nice house."

Cam wasn't worried about the house—he was worried about Rick seeing it. He had told him, several times, that it was a big house. Cam didn't think that he got it.

Cattie had told him that she had put her home on the market so that she could move closer to the two of them. She didn't live all that far, but it was about a twenty-minute drive. Their mom had already said that she'd stay wherever they wanted her to, as soon as their father was told she was leaving him. And he would be, just as soon as this was finished with the agents going down for this. Rick's mom wanted to be closer too, but not to live with them. She would need something with fewer windows for now.

At ten minutes after six Carter showed up, driving a brand-new car. When he got out of it, he pulled out his handkerchief and wiped at something on the hood. As soon as he stepped away from it, someone would go in and put a tracking device on it. The same would happen to Leon's as soon as he showed up. If, by chance, they did manage to get away, they wanted to be able to find them quickly, before they had time to leave the country.

Leon was right on the dot at six-thirty. Cam watched him. He was talking—more like yelling—about the car that Carter had bought and telling the other man how stupid he was for buying it. Then he asked about Debra, and the wife.

"All taken care of. I'll have to use a tarp next time. They bitched about having to clean up that much blood." Leon asked about the weight of the daughter. "They didn't say anything about that. Though I'm to understand that I have to call for carpet cleaning from now on rather than anything to do with dry cleaning. They're under the assumption that someone might be onto them."

Cam looked at his sister, and she gave him the thumbs up. He told her, via their link, the name of the carpet cleaning firm as well as the dry-cleaning place that was used as a front that he'd gotten from Carter's mind. She told him that she'd have them watched. And when this was over, they'd spring something on them to get them caught. This was going much better than anyone had thought. At least that's what Cam was hoping.

The trucks pulled onto the airstrip about ten minutes later. The four men, all of them agents, got out and were talking about the weather, along with the money they'd had to pay coming through Pennsylvania. Right on cue, the non-driver asked to use the bathroom.

"I don't know what there is around here. Christ man just whip it out and go over there." The man walked away with the other guy, and they were soon outfitted with jackets, guns, as well as badges. "You'd think they never did this shit before."

Leon laughed with Carter, and Cam waited until they were at the back of each of the trucks. They had used a fairly new thing by having a drone flying quietly overhead. They were not going to miss a thing. The trucks were side by side so that they'd not have to go far to look inside of them. That was what they were waiting for. And for one of them, it didn't matter which, to say something about everything being correct on the load.

The trucks were opened up, and it was a very tense few minutes as they each got inside the trucks and looked around. The pallets were filled with the same kind of dressing as had been on the other trucks, but there wasn't much tobacco beyond the first couple of layers. Cam watched as Leon nearly fell getting out of the truck, and thought it would be just like the man to break his fucking neck before they could arrest him.

"Looks good to me."

Carter took one clipboard and Leon the other. As soon as they were signed and handed back to the drivers, Cam gave the okay for all the agents to go to the two men. It was touch and go there for a couple of seconds, when it looked as if Carter was trying to get away. But they were in cuffs and down on their bellies in minutes.

"Hello, gentlemen. Remember me?" Cattie was getting the honor of letting the two of them know that they'd been caught. The cursing from the two of them was funny, while pathetic as well. "Guess what? You guys are under arrest for a long list of shit that you've been doing."

"I demand that you uncuff me this minute. I was working with the man in charge." Cattie asked who that might be. "I don't answer to you, young lady. And where have you been all this time? Did you know that everyone thinks you're dead? I didn't. I was playing with Wayne here to get him into trouble. Uncuff me right now and I'll explain."

"Deputy Carter and Leon. Who is it you've been working with if not for me?" The president laughed when they tried to tell him that they'd not had knowledge of what was going on with the trucks. "Really? Because from where I was standing, I heard you ask the driver if they could drop off a case of smokes at your home. You were going to have some early Christmas gifts to hand out."

After their rights were read to them, both men were put into the ATF vans. Not only were they cuffed, but they were chained to the seats in the back and hauled away in separate vehicles. It was a good day for a lot of people, and Cam was thrilled to death that no one was hurt.

~*~

Rick was trying very hard not to get noticed. Not that he was ashamed of being mated to Cam, never that, but he knew that this was Cam's moment, and he wanted him to have all the glory that came with it. Being invited to dinner with the president was great, and he couldn't wait to hear what the man had to say to all them about what had gone down today.

"I'm going to need someone to head up the offices there in Ohio." The president looked at Cam, then at Cattie. "Either one of you know of someone that might be good in the position?"

"Nope. You, Cattie?" She shook her head too. Everyone laughed at Cam when he told the president that he'd have a hell of a time filling the position.

"I was hoping that one of you would take it. It'll be a perfect jumping point for either of you."

"No, thanks." Cattie smiled at him with a wink. "My brother and I have just figured out that we like the life of leisure. And on top of that, there is just too much bullshit going on at my house now for me to want to go back."

"Are you going to go back to police work, Lieutenant Henderson?" Cattie told him that she was only a sergeant. "Not anymore. As of this morning, I signed off on you being promoted to lieutenant. It's the least I could do for you, after all that you went through of late."

She looked like she was going to argue, but President Wendell looked at Cam. And when he laughed, Rick was slightly confused until he spoke.

"I'm happy just where I am as well, as just Agent Henderson. I still have some things to work out in my personal life, but if and when I go back, it's going to be just plain old agent." President Wendall was shaking his head even before Cam was finished speaking. "Yes, I'm afraid that I, like my sister, am not ready for more responsibility."

"Be that as it may, you are getting the promotions. As well as all the perks that come with them. Deputy Cronkite is retiring, and I don't think I could pick a better man than you to take his place. You might just be able to shake things up a bit at the Ohio offices. What do you think?"

Rick thought that it was funny how the man just ignored both Cam and Cattie. He had them moving into the offices, with perks, as early as tomorrow, with a car in their driveways for each of them. And neither of them had ever said that they'd take the job that was being pushed through for them.

When they were on their way back to their home, he and

Cam rode in the big limo with Wendall. The man was still working on trying to convince Cam to take the job, and when he turned to him, Rick put up his hand.

"No, I'm not going to convince him to do this. The thing is, I do believe you when you say that he'd be perfect for the job. However, what you don't know is that I think he's had enough. Today—this thing from today was personal, as you well know, and the fact that it went off without trouble—that, I have to think, isn't the norm." Wendall said that it usually wasn't. "I didn't think so. But as for Cam taking the job, that would be entirely up to him. I will support him in any endeavor that he wants to do, but I won't push him into anything. I know he's a smart enough man to figure out what he wants to do when he wants to do it."

Cam held his hand and didn't say a word. It was great having someone that didn't care what even the President of the United States had to say about having a gay couple working for him. But Rick had a feeling that before this was all finished not only would Cam be working for him, but Cattie would be taking over the stationhouse where she had been working. She'd have it cleaned up in no time at all, too.

As soon as they were home, he and Cam settled in the living room with Jake and Forrest. Cattie had a date with some of her friends, while the four of them were just going to hang out until bed time. Jake asked Cam if he was going to take the job.

"No. I don't want to put myself out there again." Forrest asked him what he meant. "Well, everyday there was a nightmare for someone like me. I feel too much from everyone. I know their every thought and every move. And that can make a person crazy after a while."

"True. But wouldn't it make you a better boss? I mean, you'd know when there was trouble. You'd be in an office all day, correct?" Cam said that he more than likely would be going out too. "But you don't have to. I'd say that this would be the perfect job for you."

Rick started to tell him not to push him. The president had tried, and he wasn't having it. But Cam got up and started to pace a little before he turned back to Forrest. In his hand was not just a gun but also a knife, as well as an extra magazine for the gun. No one said a word as Cam broke down the gun and handed it to Forrest.

"Okay, do you know where I got this?" Forrest shook his head. "That was on the man that lives next door to you. Do you want to know why he had it? It was to shoot you and or Jake when you came out of the house next. I didn't go looking for it. When I put my mind out there to search for local danger, that's what came to me."

"He wanted to kill us?" Cam nodded, and the weapons disappeared. "Why? What the hell have we ever done to him? He never struck me as homophobic."

"Believe it or not, it has nothing to do with you being gay. It's because he thinks that you're running a hotel here, and he wants a piece of the income. He wants to be able to rent his home out as well. And since your home is nicer, he figured that if you were dead, he could take over where you were making a killing." Forrest didn't say anything. Cam laughed. "He won't now—I've taken care of that. But that is just a small portion of shit that I'd have to put up with."

"And you somehow think that's a bad thing? I don't mean about my neighbor—thank you for that, by the way. I just mean you feeling out where there could be danger. Think of all the in-house things you could avoid, Cam." He asked Jake want he meant. "Bear with me here a moment. My ex-wife, Carol—you guys, I'm sure, have heard of her. What kind of help do you think it would have been for me to find out earlier that she'd already murdered two people? That she'd been planning all along to have affairs in our home. For me, that would have meant a great deal. I wouldn't have been as hurt. I might still have my grandma, too, if it hadn't ended the way that it did. I can't just think of the bad things, though I'm not dismissing that for you, but all the good things that can and will come from you having advance notice on things like that."

"You're not understanding." Jake told him that he was understanding. That Cam had a little extra that could save not just the men that worked for him, but the people that they might encounter as well. "You think that I should be calling them up when I know something is going to happen to them? To monitor their every thought and every move? That was why I hated my job in the first place. And I was forever tense, so that I wasn't listening to myself and shot a kid."

"You shot a kid that was going to kill you. Even if you hadn't been stressed out, watching over everyone else, would you have known what the child was going to do to you?" Cam shook his head. "Yeah, I didn't think so. You can feel everyone else, but not you, correct?"

"Right." Cam sat down then and looked at his hands instead of Jake when he spoke again. "I've not been able to feel anything to do with anyone in this house since I've become a part of your family. And that frightens me just a little, if you want to know the truth."

"Good." Cam looked at Jake, and he smiled. "I don't want you to know everything I'm doing, thinking, or even worried about. But, and tell me if I'm wrong, would you know if I was going to be hurt? That something was going to happen to me because of someone else's thoughts?"

"Yes. Because I'm no longer stressed about what is going

to happen to me. But what the other person is — I guess you're right. I would be able to help if I were to just relax a bit." Jake nodded. "But that doesn't mean I'd be any good at the job."

"You know as well as everyone in this house that you'd be perfect for the job. The only thing holding you back is your fear of one of us getting hurt. Or that you might." Jake laughed. "You're an immortal, the same as the rest of us. Yes, we can all be hurt, but not killed. That has to take a great deal of stress from you as well. Right?"

Cam didn't say anything, but Rick could see the beginning of a smile on his face. He was caving. Or maybe not caving, but he was beginning to see himself in the position of Director of the FBI at the local level. As the rest of them kept coming up with the perks he'd have as a director, Cam started nodding. It would be a done deal soon enough, Rick would bet.

As the night wore on, he and Cam ended up in the living room alone. While they were watching something on the television, Cam started making notes about things that he'd been told. By the time they were on their way up to their room, Rick was sure that he was going to take it. It was just a matter of Cam convincing himself that he'd be perfect for the job.

The phone was ringing as they reached their bedroom. Cam answered it and put it on speaker so that he could hear as well.

"We found some things in Wayne Leon's underground house that you might be interested in. By the way, thanks for the heads up on that. It's doubtful that we would have just come across it if we didn't have prior knowledge." Cam asked Carmichael what it was that he'd found. "Notebooks, about fifty of them so far. They have every deed that he did, each job that he worked, and the conclusion of them. Also, and this is why I called you, there are several entries about Rick's father. I think we might know where to pick him up."

101

"Where is he?" Cam asked Carmichael where he might be so that Rick would know as well. "I'd like to be there too when they pull him in. He hurt my mom." Cam would be there as well. If for no other reason than to support Rick.

Arrangements were made so that the two of them would be with Carmichael when the arrest was made. Attempted murder was part of it, as well as conspiracy to kill an agent—namely Cam. Before they hung up, they were set up to meet the agent at the hotel where his father was staying. Cam asked Rick if he was sure about going.

"We might have to shoot him." Rick said that he understood. "You might see him killed, is what I'm trying to tell you."

"Have you seen it?" Cam said that he'd not looked. "Don't. I want to go if for no other reason than to see him behind bars. I'm finished with his ass."

"All right. Then we'll go and find my dad too. He's been stirring up trouble himself. And I've spoken to your mom, she is going to stay with us. She was told that she'd be all right in the sunlight."

Curling around each other in the big bed, they made plans to go and see Cam's home after dealing with Richard Whitehall. Rick wasn't sure what the big deal was about the house, but he figured that he'd find out tomorrow. He was just thrilled to be living with him. They could be in a hovel for all he cared. Tomorrow was going to be a big day for the two of them, and Rick was looking forward to it.

"By the way, I'm taking the job." Smiling, Rick told him he knew and kissed him on the mouth. "You're a jerk, anyone ever tell you that?"

They were still laughing when Cam turned out the lights. Rick was almost too excited to sleep, and that was when he realized that he no longer hurt. And he was pretty sure that

Cam didn't either. They were good for each other in a lot of ways, apparently.

Chapter 8

Richard was broke. Half a million hadn't gone nearly as far as he'd thought it would. Smiling, he remembered all the fun that he'd had when he had it. Then he thought that if he was able to find those two people, the Hendersons, the people who'd paid him would give him more. Picking up the newspaper, he had to sit down hard when he read the headlines.

"Holy fuck." They'd been arrested. The men that he'd been dealing with — well, one time, anyway — were being loaded into large vans with ATF on the side of them. Pulling the photos that had come with the article a little closer to his face, he dropped it like a hot poker. "Rick is there too."

Reading the entire article twice, he didn't see any mention of his name or that of his son. But that was him, sure as shit — that was Rick standing next to the fucking President of the United States. And in a couple of the photos he could see that Rick was shaking hands with the man. Holy fuck, his son was famous. Richard wondered if he could get any kind of money from that. His son was up and friendly with the president.

Richard caught himself strutting around the room twice. He

wasn't sure what sort of payoff he could get for this, but surely there were favors that he could grant people now that he had a son that was in good with the big man. Making himself notes, he didn't even bother with wadding the paper up and tossing it across the room this time. Folding it neatly and putting it in a drawer with his other things, he was thinking about going out and buying several copies of the paper before they were all gone.

The list was about two pages long now. He was glad for the first time since moving into the place that they gave him access to the little fridge, as well as pens and paper.

He was on his fourth beer when someone knocked on the door. Richard didn't even look this time—he was much too famous to be bothered with looking at whoever it was through the peephole.

The door crashed back on the hinges when he only just took the chain off. Falling back on his ass, he looked at the woman before him and tried to place her. It took his befuddled mind several seconds to realize that it was his wife.

"What the hell did you do to yourself, Patsy? You look amazing." He frowned when the man behind her crowded into the room. "Hey, I don't know you, nor did I invite you in. You gotta leave. My wife and I, we got shit to discuss."

"We really don't, you moron. And we don't have to be invited in since you've never made this place your own, so we don't need an invite." He wasn't sure what she was saying. "I'm a vampire, you ass wipe. Thanks to you. Not that I'm not enjoying my new life, but—"

"What the fuck do you mean you're a vampire? There isn't any such thing as bloodsuckers." Richard felt his balls tighten up to his body when she smiled at him. The man too. Christ, their fangs were as lethal looking as the knife he'd hidden in

106

his laundry yesterday. "Where did you get those? They look mighty nice, but they're not real, are they, Patsy?"

He was grasping at straws, he knew that, but she was scary looking. Not to mention the big man behind her. Richard thought that he might be able to lift cars, he was so big. Standing up, careful of where they were, he backed as far away from them as he could and still be in the same room.

"I've come to hold you here." He didn't bother saying anything. Richard knew there was no reasoning with his wife when she was in this sort of mood. "My boy is coming here soon, and I made him a promise that I'd not kill you before he arrives."

"What's he coming for? To tell me about some deal he's made with the president? I'm telling you now, Patsy, this is going to be good for us. Can you see us, up there having dinner in the Oval Office with our baby boy? I don't know that I'd mention that he's a queer. It might get him kicked out. I was—"

"They don't have meals in the Oval Office. I told you, Howard, he's a fool. The world would be a better place without him around." Howard just nodded and put his arm around Patsy's waist. Richard didn't care for his wife, not anymore, but he'd need her to get in good with Rick, so he kept his mouth shut about the man manhandling his wife. "And for the record, the president knows that he's gay, and doesn't care about it."

"I guess he'd have to say he liked everybody, don't you think? For the vote. Not that there can be that many queers around." She corrected him again. "I don't care what he calls himself, damn it, woman. I just care about what he's going to be doing when he gets here." She moved across the room— floated, more like it. And when she sat down, the big man, Howard, stood behind her.

"Why aren't you trying to hurt me, Richard? That's what

you would normally do if I invaded someplace you were. I mean, don't you want to hit me?" He asked her what she was talking about. "Well, I can kill you if you try and hurt me. I really want you to try. And this time, it will only be you trying. I'm a great deal stronger than I used to be."

"Yeah, so you said. You're a vampire." He sat down in the chair that he'd come to hate. It was smaller than he needed it to be, and he didn't care for being in a lesser position than she was. "Why does our boy want to come and see me? You got any ideas?"

"Yes. I have plenty of them. But since you asked so nicely, I'll tell you. He's coming to have you arrested." Richard leaned back in the chair, deciding that he didn't care for Patsy right now. He asked her where she'd gotten that fool reason. "You hurt me."

"I did no such a thing. You can't even prove it if I did, either." She asked him about the two men that had come to question her. "You mean those men that came to ask you where Rick was? That is not my fault that you got hurt, Patsy. You should have just answered them when they asked you shit. And if you have been reading the paper, they've been put in jail anyway. So, you should tell the people that put them there."

"But you did send them after me — didn't you, Richard? You sent them to my home and had them beat me nearly to death." He told her that she looked all right to him. "Of course, I do — I've been changed into a lovely vampire. And I have to tell you, Richard, you lied to me about sex. Women are supposed to enjoy it too. You were just a lousy lover, I guess. Not to mention, you have a very tiny dick." She put two fingers together to about half an inch apart.

"That ain't right, Patsy. Airing out our — What the hell do you mean, I lied to you? How the hell would you have figured that out? You have sex with that man behind you?"

"Oh, yes. And Quincey too. Together sometimes. Oh, my yes. Sex is a great deal more fun than you ever let me have before." He stood up, and Howard suddenly wasn't alone. There was another man with him, this one bigger than him. "Richard, I'd like for you to meet my makers, Quincey and Howard. They have no last name, which matters little to me, but they have been teaching me a great deal. More than you ever took the time to show me. But then you always were a selfish prick, weren't you? Hello, Rick. I've not hurt him as yet."

"Hello, Mom. Howard and Quincey been making you behave?"

Patsy pouted, and for the first time in his entire married life with her, and Richard was turned on. He had to adjust his cock twice, and he had a feeling that she knew just what he'd been thinking, too. Christ, she was nothing but sex on a stick, as his daddy was fond of saying about women.

"Richard Whitehall, I'm here to inform you of your rights. Sadly, I can't arrest you, but I can tell you how much you're going away for."

"Arrest me? What the hell for? I'm going to have to teach you a few things, boy. But I want to talk to you about your in with the president. Christ almighty, son. You sure have done your daddy proud. When am I going to get to meet him? I'd love to see about getting into the White House too."

"No."

He looked at Rick, then at his wife. All he'd had to do in the past was just reach for his belt and Rick would be quivering in the corner. This time all he did was laugh. "This is no way to treat your father, son."

"Why is it that I'm only your son when you need something? And I'm happy to point out, you're not going to get anything from me. Not ever again." Three more men walked in the room, all of them wearing vests like there was going to be a shoot-out at the corral or something. "These men are here to arrest you. And I'm hoping that you're going to resist, just so they can beat the shit out of you."

"Now see here." Richard was cuffed, his arms jerked up behind him without any thought to how painful it might be to him. These men were not nice, and Richard thought about pointing out to them how he knew the president. Even as he opened his mouth, he was read his rights. "What are you doing? I'm telling you right now, I'm not going to stand for this. I've done nothing wrong. Tell them, Patsy. Tell them how I had nothing to do with you being nearly killed."

She only laughed at him, and he began to see where he might not be getting out of this like he'd thought. Not even asking his boy why he didn't tell them who he was, who he knew. They were taking him out the door when he realized that he was fucking going to jail. And he still hadn't any idea why.

"You do know." He looked at the man in front of him. His picture had been in the paper too, right alongside of his boy. "And thankfully, I know too. You haven't been a good father, much less a good human being, have you, Richard? And on top of all the things we did know about you, I'm happy to tell you that it's not even the tip of the iceberg on what we know now."

It was confusing, but as he began to listen to the charges, he knew that someone had sold him out. And he had a feeling that it had been his own family. Christ almighty, didn't anybody care about loyalty, or even family anymore? As he was being taken to the police van just outside the hotel, the manager of the hotel, the one that had offered him the suite of rooms he was in now when he had money, was handing the stranger a sheet of paper. No doubt the bill. He wasn't going to pay that either, he told them.

"Oh, but you will, Father. And when we figure out where you've parked your new car, as well as the crap that you felt you needed, we're going to use that as payment on a lot of things." The other man, he'd called him Cam, told Rick where the car was. How the hell were they finding this shit out? "Thanks, Cam."

Then his boy did the most revolting thing he'd ever witnessed. He went over and kissed Cam on the mouth. It was making him ill, it was, the way that they moaned and shit— like they were enjoying it or something. There wasn't a bit of human decency in people anymore. And having the queers running around like real people was the ruination of the world.

Richard was out in the van when he realized that no one had answered him about going to the White House. He wasn't sure that Patsy was right about them not eating in the Oval Office. He only wanted to eat in there because it seemed to him that was where all the cameras were. And he really wanted someone to take his picture in that room with the president. Trying to think what the man's name was, he was in a jail cell before he could remember. It was Windbag, he thought. Well, if that wasn't his name, Richard thought that it was a perfect one for him. The man was forever interrupting his favorite shows talking about stuff nobody cared about.

"Hey, when you see my boy, can you ask him to come see me? He never told me when I was going to the big house with him." The officer that was locking him in said that Rick wasn't coming in. "Sure he is. I'm sure that he's going to bail me out of this. Can't have me sitting in here while he's making plans with the big man. I might even forgive him for being a queer if he treats me right."

The man just walked away. Richard had a feeling that

he was one of them too. The world was being overrun with weirdos. Well, his son would get on the bandwagon soon. He'd have to soon enough. President Windbag wasn't going to be putting up with that stuff either.

~*~

Cam was in the living room waiting on Rick. He'd been wandering off from him in the house since they'd arrived. He figured that he was going to come back and say something like he couldn't live here, it was just too monstrous, and they'd buy something different. Cam didn't care so long as they were together.

Wilbur joined him in the room. "The staff and I have done as you've asked, sir. All the things that had been in the closets have been sent out to the cleaners. Also, the gardens and the pool house have been gone over as well. We know that the outdoor pool won't be used for a few months, but the indoor one is ready for use." Cam thanked him. "If I might ask, sir, do you plan to sell if the young man isn't happy here? If so, the staff and I have talked it over, and we'd very much like to go with you to your new home."

"Thanks, Wilbur. That's very nice of you. But that'll be up to Rick. Do you know where he is now?" He said that he thought he was on the upper levels. "All right. I was thinking that we'd have dinner here tonight. Cattie will be joining us. Are there provisions to make something for us to have? It doesn't have to be elaborate."

"We stocked up." Wilbur grinned. "We were hoping that we might have one more big meal here before you might have to sell. Do you believe that he'll be unhappy here?"

Before Cam could answer him, Rick came into the room. He just stood in the doorway, looking around this room again. Cam started to laugh, but decided that he'd wait to see how he was taking this all in.

"I counted fourteen bedrooms in this place." He said that there were two in the sublevels as well, and a cook's home. "Yes, because I needed to know that. And there are nineteen bathrooms. Not counting the ones in the basement or the cook's house. Did you know that there is an elevator too?"

"Yes. I did, as a matter of fact." Rick nodded and walked around the room. "There is an outdoor and an indoor greenhouse at the back of the property as well. I believe that the cook uses it year-round to have fresh herbs for meals. We'll be having dinner here tonight, if that's all right with you."

"Sure. Is this a Rembrandt?" Cam said that it was. "And how much money did you pay for that? Never mind. I don't think I could take it. I was noticing as well that there is a fitness room, and I think I saw a running track around the trees in the back."

"There is. It's five miles." Rick just glared at him, and Cam laughed. "You're overwhelmed, aren't you? I don't blame you. When I bought this place, I was under the assumption that the ad in the paper was incorrect when it said that the house was sixty-seven thousand square feet. I thought, surely it's not that large."

"But it was." Cam nodded and patted the seat beside him. "Not just yet. I have questions. First one is, why did you think that I'd not like it here? The size? That surely is a big thing to get used to."

"I agree. It took me having a map made up so that I could find my way around." Rick wandered around the room again. "What else did you want to know?"

"You told me that you bought this house sight unseen. Why was that?" He told him that he'd been out of country when his attorney told him that a house had come onto the market, and that it would be a good investment, especially at the price it was. "And was it cheaper than about six million?"

"It was about half that, really." Rick stopped moving around and stared at him. "I was told that it was built for a very wealthy man and his entire family, thus all the bedrooms. But something happened, and the house needed to be taken off the bank's books. I was in the right place at the right time, you might say."

"How did that happen?" Cam didn't want to tell him, but he asked him again. "You knew the man and his family?"

"Sort of. I was responsible for his death. He wasn't anyone that needed to be walking around any longer. I didn't take out his family—he'd done that a few hours before we raided his home. I told you that I was in the service before I became an agent."

"Yes…yes you did." Rick sat down. "The staff that is here, did they come with the house or were they someplace else as well?"

"My parents' home. Before my father lost everything." Rick nodded, and Cam didn't see any reason to continue. "Cattie and I bought this place, and when she found herself something, I bought her out. She has a home just over in Trinway, but I think she's planning to sell it as well."

"I want to live here." Cam felt the breath he'd not realized he was holding whoosh out of his lungs. "When I first saw the place, even from the driveway, I thought this was not a place for someone like me to live. It's a rich man's home."

"You are a rich man, Rick. Simply because I am. What I have is yours." Rick nodded, looking around the room. Cam waited for him to deny it. "Do you think you could be happy here? I mean, I know that you said that you wanted to live here, but do you think you'll be happy here, with me?"

"I do. Very happy. I can see us having holidays here. Having my mom and yours here with the rest of them. This room alone would be fantastic decorated for any holiday, but especially Christmas." Cam said that he'd never decorated this house for any holiday. "You ever live here?"

"Yes, for about a year. I was alone though. Well, the servants were here, but I was out of work and hurting bad enough that I wasn't having fun. The pool went untouched. The sauna room, which you didn't mention, wasn't used. I was just a very lonely man living in a house that needed a family. And I'd very much like to have one with you." Rick said that he wanted that as well. "Good. I'm so glad to hear that from you. When do you think you'd be ready to move in?"

"Today?" Cam laughed again. "I don't have anything. Not that you need anything to fill out the rooms, but I don't have— Please don't tell me what you have I have. I'm overwhelmed enough. I have to ask you this. I know that I'll regret it, but just how much are you...we worth?"

"Fifty billion, not including stocks that we have. That's just this house and the others that I own." Rick leaned back on the couch and closed his eyes and asked him what else. "We have a few homes overseas—one in every country, as a matter of fact. I've been very lucky with the stock market. Perhaps because of this thing I can do, but I saw no reason not to use it if I could. I've made more money in one week than most make in—"

"Enough." Cam laughed. "You are enjoying this a little too much, I think. What if I hadn't liked the house? What would you have done with it? I don't think there is a market in Ohio for a home this large."

"No, there isn't. But there are lots of things that could have been done to it should you have not wanted to live here. A hotel comes to mind. A bed and breakfast too. As you pointed out, there are plenty of bedrooms and bathrooms here." Rick nodded and reached for his hand. Cam gladly took it into his own. "Quincey and Howard are going to live in the lower levels with your mom. She's taken to the house much better than you did."

"My mom is so different that I almost don't know her anymore. I think that's because someone really loves her." Cam said that helped. "She's also more confident than I've ever known her to be, don't you think?"

"I would say that's about right. My mom is moving in when we decide where to put her. I was going to ask Wilbur if he had any use for the house outback—the cook's home—and see if she wanted to live there." Rick asked why Wilbur didn't live there. "He has a few rooms on this floor that he likes. Wilbur is a wolf, and when the need comes to him, he goes out to roam with the others here."

"You've always been wealthy, haven't you? I mean, the reason that I say that is because you seem so comfortable with all this. You are, aren't you?" Cam told him that his grandparents had money that they shared with him and Cattie. "Are they still living? I mean, I have no one but my mom—and my dad, I suppose—in blood relatives."

"Cattie and I have a grandfather that drops in when he wants. He usually stays for a few months before he needs to move on again. I have a grandmother—they're not related—that comes to visit as well. She doesn't want to intrude, so she has been staying in a hotel. You'll love them both. My grandmother on my father's side and my grandfather on my mom's died when I was younger. They were very wonderful people too."

"No doubt." Wilbur joined them to ask if anyone else was coming to dinner. Rick asked if Cam's mom would be joining them, and Cam said that he'd ask. "Why don't we have them all over? I mean, the entire family of queers, as my father is so fond of calling us."

Calls were made, and everyone agreed to come to dinner. Wilbur and the staff were happy with the turn of events, and Cam could smell pies being made, as well as bread. It was going to be a comfort food dinner, if he didn't miss his bet. By the time they'd gone over the house again, this time with one of the housemaids, they had a long list of things that they would need. Towels, as well as personal items for the house to be brought in.

"I've never done anything more than just stay here. It'll be fun making it a home with you." Rick agreed as he looked at the master bedroom. Dismissing the maid, Cam watched her leave them in the room. "We're going to need a bigger bed, I think. And did you notice the nursery down the hall?"

"I did. And I'm not sure when we should work on filling that part of the house, but we can be looking." Rick sat on the side of the bed. "How about we break this in? I mean, it might be just big enough for the two of us. Surely, we should try it out, don't you agree?"

"I do, as a matter of fact." Cam moved to the bed and was stopped by Rick. He told him that he wanted this to be special. "No, not going to happen, I'm sorry to say. But I've been wanting to see you naked here since we pulled in front. So, if you don't mind, we can be special later."

They were both laughing as they stripped. It wasn't just a removal of clothing, but literal. Everything was in rags on the floor, and all Cam could think about was that it was a good thing they could dress magically. Otherwise they'd be naked when company showed up.

Chapter 9

Rick just loved to touch Cam. His skin was warm—not hot, just a comfortable warm. His chest was furred. He thought that he might enjoy that the most, as his own chest was smooth, but they were both hard, and what most would call packed. And since they'd been sleeping in the same bed, though not so much sleeping as touching and being together, they both had commented on how much better they were feeling. Rick had even given up taking pain pills. No matter what they'd been doing during the day, it no longer seemed to affect the way he felt. Nor did he hurt any longer.

"You have the most beautiful eyes when you're aroused." Cam grinned at him, and said that they must be beautiful all the time, as he was always aroused when Rick was nearby. "Yeah, well, there is that."

He enjoyed the way Cam was hesitant when touching him. Never taking too much, just making him feel loved and wanted. And when he kissed him, it was like he was being refueled, his body being overcharged every time the two of them were together like this.

"I've been wanting to taste you since yesterday when you woke me up with your mouth." Cam moaned, and that was all it took for Rick to feel his cock stretch, his balls fill to a painful point. "Your mouth is so wonderfully talented. I love you."

They caressed each other, fingers moving over muscles with gentle hands. From the start, Cam had been the one who would touch the most. It was something that Rick had looked forward to all day. And when Rick took Cam's cock into his hand, he dropped to his knees in front of his lover and watched him as Rick's fist moved up and down.

"I thought this was going to be quick." Rick told Cam that was his idea, not his. "Yes, well, I think I like this so much better. And as much as I don't want to rush you, we do have company coming in two hours."

"Plenty of time for me to make you scream." He nearly fell back when he took Cam's cock into his mouth. The way Cam fucked his mouth, he knew that he'd be sore later, but he was enjoying himself too much to have him slow down. Holding onto his nice firm ass, Rick made love to his cock as Cam had done for him that morning, making him come three times before they'd had a shower.

"You're killing me, Rick. I want to come so badly, but I want this to last, too." He wasn't in any rush to make him come. Rick was enjoying himself too much for this to stop. "I need to be inside of you. Please. I need you badly."

Letting Cam's cock fall from his mouth, he licked the precum off the tip, then moaned again when he swallowed. There wasn't anything better than Cam's cum. And when he was helped up from the floor, Cam had him get up on the bed so that he could take him.

They'd only been making love this way for a few days. It had been painful for them both—neither of them had a small cock. But the feeling of having Cam moving inside of him made Rick's cock burn with desire. And when he was seated, Cam laid his head on his back and kissed him there.

Rick took his own cock in his hand when Cam started to fuck him. It was slow going, but as soon as he got his rhythm, Rick was holding on to his cock and the bed for all he was worth. And when Cam reached down and took Rick's cock in his own hand, Rick watched his hand moving quickly and tightly up and down his cock even as he filled him.

When he was ready to come, Cam pulled him up from his position and bit hard on his neck. It was a sensation that Rick had never felt before, and when Cam sucked hard on the wound that he'd made, Rick felt his cock explode just as Cam filled him with his own release.

Neither of them stopped. Cam suckled at his throat while his cock filled again. Rick was dizzy with the need to come a third time, and when his lover gave over his wrist to him, Rick felt his own teeth explode through his gums as he felt the need to bite back. As soon as he did, Rick came a fourth then a fifth time, making his vision not just blur, but blink out.

When Rick woke he was still on the bed, Cam behind him, talking softly to him. When Rick turned to look at Cam, he was rewarded with a kiss that was both deep and delicious. They held each other for several minutes before Cam moved back. He never let him go, holding him in his arms until they decided it was time to get ready for their guests.

They showered together, washing each other's back and chest, kissing and touching wherever they could reach. And when he washed Cam's long hair, all he could think about was that he was so lucky he was going to be able to do this every day for the rest of their lives.

Getting dressed was even fun. Neither of them had to worry

about what to wear. They just thought of what they wanted, and it appeared on them. Rick was a jeans and shirt sort of man, while Cam was just as casual in his dress. He was happy with sweat pants, T-shirt, and socks. No shoes, he told Rick, as they didn't feel right.

Laughing, they decided that the closet needed to have something in it, even if it was just for show for the people that did work for them. The two of them decided that while they were out looking for items to fill the house, they'd pick up a few things for themselves.

Going down the stairs to the main level of the house, they found Wally waiting for them. The man was forever smiling, and in turn it made anyone around him smile as well.

"I have me some news for you both. My goodness, you sure do look like a happy couple." Rick told him that they were, and if it was bad news, to not give it to them now. "No, not bad at all. But it is something that you should be made aware of. There be a ghost here with you. I don't think you know her—she's new to even me. But she wants to ask you a few questions about the house."

Rick wasn't sure that he would be able to answer anything and started away to check on dinner. But Wally called him back, as this was a question that they both should answer. The ghost, Madeline, wanted to know if she could stay with them.

"Why here?" Rick looked at Cam when Wally glanced in the direction he assumed Madeline was standing. "I mean, I don't know anyone by that name. Do you?"

"No, I don't think so." Wally reached out and touched the woman, and she appeared before them. "No, I'm sure I don't know her. Do you know us?"

"Nay, my lord. But I am aware of you." He asked her what she meant. "You have taken care for us, the ones that had been victims of the monster, that he will no longer be free to kill anyone else. That is more than we could have hoped for."

"Who would that be?" She didn't know his name, but he'd killed her along with a couple of other women. He was a masochist. "Is his name Wayne Leon?" He reached into her mind. Even though she was no longer living, he could see the man's face. "Yes, that's him. I'm sorry for your death, my dear. But you've not answered us as to why here?"

"There are others here. Some of them belonged to the house — the builders that the master killed when they were not working as hard as he wished. There are a couple of them, much older than even Wally here, that are out in the barn, just waiting for someone to move into this house so that they might be a part of it." Rick wasn't sure what to think about that. He really didn't have an opinion one way or the other and told Cam that. "We will cause you no harm, my lords. There is another, Miss Christy, that Wally has said is a good soul, and is willing to teach some of us."

"You can read." She said that she could read some, not much, but she couldn't write. Her family had seen no reason for her to learn either, as she was just going to be helping on the farm. "I see. And you think that Christy can help you?"

"Yes, my lord. She has told Mr. Wally that she will help any of us, so long as we follow the rules of the dead. There are so many of them, but we have checked and she isn't breaking any by teaching us to do some things." Rick said that they'd have to get a list of the rules for themselves if they were going to have guests. "There is a copy for anyone to read, the living or dead, that each of us have. I will be happy to lend you my copy so that you will know that we're not breaking them."

"All right then. I don't have a problem with you staying here so long as you cause us no trouble." Rick nodded at Cam's statement. "Also, there are others here, living, that I wish for you to make yourself known too. Three of them are vampires."

"We have no trouble with the living dead, sir. It's the living humans that we usually have troubles with." Rick asked her what sort of trouble. "They walk through us. Not only that, but they curse us when they do something on their own. I do not care to be blamed for someone's clumsiness."

"No, I don't think I'd care for that either." Cam put out his hand and Madeline just stared at it. "I don't know if I can touch you or not, but I'd very much like to have a connection. And if we find anything in your pasts that broke any laws, we'll ask you or that person to leave. Understood?"

"Yes, my lord. There are many of us that have broken some laws. Not here, but we have. I had several tickets for walking wrong." She said she forgot the name it was called, and he told her. "Yes, jaywalking. And when I was very poor, I would steal a meal or two for myself. If you wish to make me leave, I will understand."

"No, not for keeping yourself fed. Jaywalking is something that I've done as well." Rick looked at Cam before continuing. "You will learn that we're very forgiving on some things, others not so much. You tell anyone that wishes to live here that they must be honest, and we'll consider them family. All right?"

"Yes, my lord." She was smiling at him, and that was when he was able to see what Leon had done to her to cause her death. "Once you have accepted us, you will be shown what our suffering was in our life. But you can make it gone, should you wish. You only need to tell us to cover it up."

"No, I don't think I'd like that either. You were hurt by a terrible man, and I'm sorry for that. Now, we're having guests tonight. Christy will be with them." Cam said that she was going to be watching over Jenna. "Good. Jenna can see you as well. She's just a baby."

"Yes, we have heard of the child. I am looking forward to seeing her as well." She started to fade out, but came back. "You have only to ask, my lords, and we'll come to your aid. Some of the others are very old and can do many things. You will be protected by us, this I make as a promise to you."

When they were gone, Rick turned to Cam and said he was sorry. "For what? You mean allowing them to come here to stay? You live here too. You can do whatever you want, and I'll support you all the way. I think I might like having a few ghosts around, don't you?"

"I don't have any idea. I think — no, I know that everything with you is going to be an adventure." Cam said that he thought so as well. "Tomorrow when we go see your father, I don't know that your sister should come. I think she might just pull out her gun and blow him away before we even get to have a talk with him."

"Would that be so bad?"

They were both still laughing when their guests started to show up. Yes, Rick thought, life was going to be more than an adventure. It was going to be a flipping blast.

~*~

Dinner was much better than they'd thought it would be. Not that the food wasn't wonderful, but just having them all together was more than Cam could have hoped for. Even Jenna, who was just now holding her bottle on her own and eating small bites of food, made everyone laugh when she found something to her dislike.

After dinner, Cam and the rest of them retired to the living room. They were a motley group — lawyers, writers, agents, cops, and actors. Then there was the fact that none of them were human anymore. When Wilbur came to tell him he had a phone call, Cam knew that it was either going to be his father, whom he'd talked to this morning to set up a time to talk to him face to face, or it was going to be the Agency.

"I was wondering why everyone is at the big house and no one invited me?" Cam told his father that he wasn't welcome. "That's no way to talk to your father, Cameron. I'm the one that is responsible for you being on this earth. The very least you could do is be grateful for that. And if you could send a little cash my way, I'd be forever grateful. You know how it is—a man doesn't have much in the way of pride when he's down on his luck."

"Yes, I'm sure you would be grateful, but I'm not a grateful child. Did you know that I spoke to Grandda Henderson today? He told me that I should have had you killed years ago. That's a great thing to have to say about your son. Oh, I forgot, you've said worse about me." Rick came into the room with him, and he let him listen on the conversation by putting it on speakerphone. "And also, you might like to be aware that Grandma Jamison is on her way here. We're going to have a houseful in a couple of days."

"Why the hell would you want those old bats there? Christ, Cameron, they'll be telling you all kinds of nasty stories about me." Cam asked him if they'd be true. "I doubt it. My father has never liked me, even before Mom passed away. And Ann, your mother's mother, isn't the least bit nice to me either. I don't want them to be around when I come for a visit."

"No one invited you to come for a visit, unless you mean someone else's house. You're not welcome here. Never, Father. I don't want you to darken my doorway again. And I do believe that I've said that to you several times in the past. You aren't going to be welcome anywhere around the family—not after what you've done. As I said to you earlier, I'll come to talk to you tomorrow, but I'm not bringing you cash." He asked what he'd done to deserve such treatment. "Well, first of all, you gambled away all the inheritance that belonged to Cattie and I. Then there was the theft of the car that you tried to blame on me. Next time get your facts right. I wasn't even in the country when you did that. And you spelled my name wrong."

"Honest mistake. But I needed a ride, and you and your sister were being selfish. I know that both of you have money. Did you see this month's copy of the rich and famous? You've dropped down to second on the list. The only person that is higher than you is some ass called Winslow." Cam told him that they were good friends. "Of course, you are. Why not? All the rich and selfish should hang together. I want you to slide me some cash, Cameron. I'm in a bad way, and I could use a few thousand to get me by. You should want me to be flush. Damn it, I'm your father."

"No." His dad started cursing and Cam laughed at him. "What a mouth you have on you, Father. Have you kissed your dad with that mouth lately? I bet he'd be shoving soap in your mouth if you did. That is what he did to you as a child, isn't it? I heard that you don't care much for the spring flavors, either."

"See what I mean? Right there, that's what I'm talking about. They never once shoved anything in my mouth. Unlike you, who would put anyone in your mouth." Cam grinned at Rick when he laughed. "Who is that? You letting people hear our private conversations, Cameron? That's not at all nice of you. Tell them to go away so we can talk."

"I think we're finished. Not just with this conversation, but with any kind of family relationship. After tomorrow, I never want to see you again. I don't like you." He heard his dad stuttering about that, and Cam laughed again. "What? You don't like to hear the truth? You've been so good at passing around so many untruths about me, it's a wonder that anyone wants to stay with me. Father, you'll be happy to know that I've found my mate. His name is Rick Whitehall. He's the best thing that has ever happened to me."

"A man? I thought you were over that shit. Cameron, you're not seeing the big picture. How the hell do you expect to make it in life if you are forever telling everyone that you're a homo?" He told his father that he was going far, even with the stigma of being a homo, as he called him. "What? You're going to be a playboy? Lazing around the house eating another man? Christ, that sickens me to even say that."

"Then don't. I don't care. And I have a job. I'm the head of the FBI unit here in Ohio. FBI District Director is my title, and I'm making things happen on my end of the world. You'd better start cleaning up your life — I'm the one that can make it a living hell for you if you don't." Again, his father was speechless. "The president is very proud of the work I've done. And I think I'll be very good at the job."

"What the fuck is this world coming to when they'll just let anyone come in and be directing decent people? I'm telling you right now, Cameron, you're never going to make it in the world if you keep letting on that you're a homo." Cam didn't say anything. What would be the point? "Are you there, or are you kissing up on that man of yours?"

"Not at the moment, no. And I've only just decided that I'm not coming to see you tomorrow. I'll send some of my staff to pick you up." He asked him what the hell he was talking about. "Non-payment of taxes, for starters. Scamming people out of their pensions. There is a long list of crap that you're going to be arrested for."

"You can't do that. And would you like to know why? Because how would that look, you being the *supposed* director of some shit job?" His father laughed hard, like the thought of him being arrested was amusing. "You tell your staff, or whatever the hell you're calling them, that I'll be waiting right here for them. And if they so much as knock on the door, I'm going to be blowing their fucking asses to hell. Just where I hope you end up, you ungrateful shithead."

The line went dead, and before Cam could throw the phone across the room, just as he was intending to do, Rick took the phone from him and put it back on the cradle. Neither of them said a word for several moments. Cam could feel his temper getting the best of him.

"Take a deep breath." He shook his head at his sister. He'd not even realized that she'd entered the room, he'd been so pissed. "Cam don't make me have to slap you. I will, you know. I'm much meaner than you are."

"You're nothing of the sort. I just had a conversation with Father." Rick called his father an ass, and Cattie agreed. "He just threatened the Agency. Surely there is something that can be done about that. I need to get brought up on all the rules. I'm sure that he can spend a long time in jail, just for that."

"Yes. But here is what I'm going to do. I'm going to go and get him." Cam was shaking his head at Cattie. Rick went behind him and started to massage his shoulders as Cattie continued. "Oh, but I am. An officer has to be with your men when they go there. And I'm going to be front and center when he tries his bullshit. You are going to go to your office, await my call that I've had to kill the prick, and we'll be happily ever after."

"I don't think that's a good idea." Cattie crossed her arms over her chest and tapped her foot. "That has never worked on me. And the reason that I think this is a bad idea is a good one. You get to kill him, and I don't."

They were still laughing when they entered the living room

again. Jake, being an attorney with Forrest, told him that he was well within his rights to have his father arrested for attempted murder of an agent. But killing him, in his opinion, was a much better idea.

It was settled. Forrest would go with her to make sure that everything was on the up and up. They would, if he allowed, arrest him. Cam had a feeling that he was going to be shot, if not killed. His father had always thought he was above such things as the law. Then at the end of the day, everyone would be happy and their fathers, both sets, would be out of their lives.

Going to bed that night, Cam felt like he could sleep for a month. As he and Rick settled into the bed, they began talking about the plans for the next day. Cam really did need to get his office set up and paperwork done as well. But it wouldn't take him all that long, and then he was coming home to await his grandparents.

Grandda and Grandma had already told him that they were going to stay for a little while. He was looking forward to that. They both had a heart of gold, and he was excited for them to meet Rick. Cattie was nervously excited to see them both as well. The two of them had always been there for he and Cattie, and he didn't foresee anything being different this visit.

As he closed his eyes, he decided that he was going to try and convince them to stay forever this time. But knowing them, they'd either have it all set up or they'd have plane tickets to someplace they were headed next and would only stay for a few days.

The next morning, by the time he got up Rick had already left. He was going to help Paddy today with his book and told Cam that he'd be home later so that they could get some things done. His sister was with Jake, making their plans. Cam was headed to his own office.

Going out to the car, he looked at the old barn at the back of Henry and Paddy's property. All the properties seemed to be butting up against each other, and that made it nice so that they could easily visit each other. The barn was a dark blood red, old and faded in places, but the roof of it, what he could see of it, was a tin one, the lightning rods dark with age as well. Cam took off his tie and made his way there now. Something — he had no idea what — was drawing him to the place, and he didn't figure that anyone would miss him for a couple of hours.

The things stored in the big empty cavern of a place were being sorted. They'd hired some of the high school kids to go through it all and sort it out as to what was going to be kept. So far, it looked as if they'd made a big dent in the crates and trucks and looking at the things he decided that he wouldn't want to help out. Most of the stuff that he could see was paperwork and Christmas items.

A few of the ornaments might be worth something, as old as they looked, but Cam was drawn to the back of the building. Going there now, he sat on the ground, leaning against the barn door. Cam looked out over the fields.

Fall was coming soon. Some of the trees had already started turning, and from here Cam could see a few trees that he thought he might like to ask for for Christmas. There was a great deal of underbrush, and he could see the tips of some of the grave markers that he'd been told were back here. Closing his eyes, he let the magic of the place, the natural magic of it, roll over him. And in seconds, Cam felt the draw of sleep come over him.

Chapter 10

"Doctor Downs, there's a call for you. It sounds like your mom again." Brody nodded and looked down at the chart that he had in his hand. "She's on line three. And she told me to tell you that if you don't talk to her now, she's coming down here with curlers in her hair and her bathrobe on. The fuzzy pink one."

Brody laughed with his nurse. What she didn't understand was, his mom would do just that. As soon as he walked to the nurses' station, he tried to think when the last time was that he'd actually spoken to his mom. It had to have been at least a week. Things were not going well for him at the moment, and while he loved his mom, he didn't want her to say she'd told him so.

Picking up the phone, he could hear her talking to someone in the room with her. Something about finding the robe. He laughed, and she scolded him for taking so long. Brody told her that he loved her.

"I love you as well. And I'm a little upset with you. Did you know that Rachel called here and told my staff that she's

133

leaving you? Please tell me that you let her." He said that he had. "Good for you. My goodness, that woman is a horror."

"She is filing for divorce as we speak." The nurses at the desk clapped their hands. "Everyone here is excited to have her out of their lives as well. She has been causing me some trouble."

"I would bet that she has. What happens to that angel of yours? I'm telling you right now, Brody, if you let that wretched woman take him from you, I'm going to beat your bottom." Brody felt his heart swell with love. His son was his world. Jordan was the only thing that was good from his marriage of ten years. "Brody, please tell me that you're going to fight for custody of him. I love that little boy as much as I do you. Most of the time."

"She is going to fight me for him because she signed a prenup and there won't be any kind of alimony from me. But child support I might have to pay if she wins." Mom told him not to lose. "Yes, well, you know as well as I do that I work a lot of hours, and that might be what she gets me on."

Brody hadn't told anyone that Jordan wasn't his. He'd known that almost as soon as he'd been born. And doing a quick test on him at birth hadn't been that hard, not as a doctor in the same hospital.

"I'll come and live with the two of you." She'd be perfect for the two of them. "You've been asking me for years to come and stay. And I might have had it not been for that whore."

"Mom, I can't talk to you here." She told him she was sorry, she'd not thought of that. "It's fine. Why don't you come over for dinner tonight? Jordan and I are going to have burgers on the grill, and you can join us."

"Brody, I can hire you an attorney if you need for me to." He told her that he could afford it. "Yes, I know that well, but you might not get the right one. Let me put some feelers out, and I'll see what I can find. Surely there are a couple of them that aren't too lazy."

He thought of the man he'd gone to college with. Jake Winslow had been begging him to come and see him for a while now. And he also said that he needed his expertise at the new clinic that he was opening up. It had been tempting before, but now, it seemed like a godsend.

"Mom, do you remember Jake, that man that I brought home a couple of times for dinner?" She said that she did, and asked about his nasty wife. "I believe that she's dead. I think that's what I read recently. Anyway, he's been asking me to come there for a visit, and to help him out with his clinic and manage it for him. I'll contact him when I get home today."

"Wonderful. Wait until I get there. I'd like to see what he has to say. Oh, Brody, this is wonderful news all around. I'll bring us some celebratory cookies over. Does Jordan still love peanut butter ones?" Brody told her that she knew he did — she loved him, so he would. "I'll stop by and pick some up. And I'll come early so I can spend some time with him. Is that all right?"

"You know that it is."

After hanging up, Brody felt better, for the first time since he'd come home two months ago to find that Rachel was having an affair. In his home. In the bed that he'd not shared with her since his son had been born.

Taking the chart with him, he entered the room he'd been avoiding all day — his father-in-law's. David Sharp had been a burr up his ass since he'd been a kid, and the man had not mellowed out since then. And he was a drunk.

"It's about time you made it in here. I've been waiting on you all day to come in and release me. Damned place doesn't have a decent meal, nor does it allow you to have a smoke when you want one." He told him he could have gone outside. "Sure. And while I'm out there, you'll have some bastard roll me. The stupidest thing that my daughter could have done was become married to you. Christ."

"You'll be happy to know that she's filing for divorce." David started to cheer, and he had to hold his head. "I would have released you yesterday, but you were too drunk to have stood up, much less taken a cab home."

"I have a damned car I could have taken." Brody had taken the keys from his clothing when he arrived. Also, the police were waiting to talk to David before he was released. "When are you going to take these damned stitches out? I've had enough of you trying to make me look bad."

"You've done a bang-up job of that all by yourself. I just put them in, all fifty-six of them. And the police are outside your room. They'd like a word or two with you about damage done to—"

"You mother fucker." Brody was thinking that this day could not be any shittier, and just let David scream at him for calling the cops. "You'd just love to see me down, wouldn't you? Christ, it's nothing. I will pay for it."

Hearing the commotion from David, the officer came into the room. Asking if he was needed, Brody left the room in favor of anything. Even having his teeth drilled out would have been better than hearing the man try to talk his way out of jail time. Brody hoped that he would be there for the next fifty years, but that wasn't going to happen.

David had not just driven through someone's yard, but he'd also hit their fence, knocked over their fountain, as well as done damage to their new car. Brody knew that David was going to try and say it wasn't him, but the moron had left his car there with his keys in it when he'd stumbled down the road.

After him falling in the middle of the road, someone had called an ambulance for him and he'd been brought in just as Brody was leaving for the night.

The rest of the morning into the afternoon was much better. He was at his offices at two, and only had one appointment to see. Mrs. Little was one hundred and four years old, and the sweetest, most cantankerous old woman that he'd ever had the pleasure of having as a patient.

Mable still got around well enough, had all her teeth, which she was extremely proud of, and had outlived nine husbands — another point that she was proud of. As soon as she walked into his offices, he could hear her telling his nurse that she'd shit, not pooped or had a bowel movement, but that she'd shit. And that it had been a good one, too. He came into the little room where she was seated on his stool and not on the bed.

"If you think I got it in me to hop up on that contraption, then I don't think I need you as a doc. If I got that much gumption, then I'm gonna go home and hump the neighbor. He's a might sweet on me." He told her he was as well. "Don't be flirting with me, Doc Brody. I know you got yourself a wife and kid. Well, you got him in your house. He's not yours, I'm betting."

"No, he's not. And the wife filed for divorce yesterday. How are you doing besides having a good poop?" She stared at him for a full minute, and he let her. "She said that I'm not giving her what she needs."

"Nah, she's getting that from everything with a peter around that place you live. What you gonna do now?" He told her his plan, the one that involved his mom and Jake. "You should do it. I've been hanging around this old world waiting on you to get yourself a clue or something. Where is the old bitch now?"

"Her parents' house. And her father is in the hospital for

a hit and run accident that the cops are investigating." She laughed, a hee-haw that sounded much like a donkey would bray. "Yes, my feelings exactly."

After giving her a once over and asking about the sore he found on her leg, he sat on the floor to have a look at her feet. He was concerned, he told her, about the swelling in her ankles, as well as the two sores he'd found on her leg.

"That sugar is a killer, you know that. And if you ask me if I'm being careful of what I eat, I'll tell you what I said the last time. Hell no, I'm not." She put her hand on his cheek, and he could feel the fragility of her bones. "Brody, you should find yourself someone and find a place that you like. Raise that boy to be a good man. There ain't no cause for him to be stuck in the house while that mom of his entertains with her body."

"What would I do without you? You just tell me like it is." She said that someone had to, he was a bit dense in the noodle. "Yes, well, I guess I am. But I'm going to see a friend of mine, at least talk to him a little, about what is going on, and see if he does divorce law. I'm sure that if he doesn't, he knows someone."

"You do know that I'll not be able to go with you, don't you? I mean, I love you like a son, but I'm telling you right now, I'm not gonna sell my house to a stranger for him to pretty it all up with modern shit that ain't no more useful than the shit I have in my house now." Brody kissed her on the cheek as he stood up. "Brody, I'm not kidding you, son. You need to get away from this place and start yourself off good. At least without that cunt no more."

"Mabel, what a mouth you have on you." She puckered up and he kissed her quickly. "I have some things to work out. So that means I'll be around for your next birthday."

"No, you go on and get yourself a house and put some

people in there that you can love. I'm telling you, son, you deserve it more than most I know." He told her that he'd be all right. That he'd bounce back on his feet. "I know you will. I do know that much about you."

When he was finished telling her what she needed to do, things he knew as surely as she did that she'd ignore every bit of it and would, on her way home, pick up a dozen donuts, as well as the little cigars that she loved to smoke. Christ, if he lived to be as old as her, Brody would more than likely be doing what he wanted too.

"I got no one left, you know that." He said that he did. "And that little nurse you been telling me to take on, she is gonna start today. That was another thing I wanted you to know. I don't want to be dead for too long before someone calls in the meat wagon to take me away. Now, you do what I tell you, and I'll be waiting for you up there near the Pearly Gates. You and me, we need to be going through there at the same time. That'll give them all something to talk about."

He was still laughing off and on about her when he had two more people come in later that day. Around four o'clock, they'd not had anyone come in for about an hour. It was usually his rounds day, Thursday, but since he'd gotten rounds at the hospital done early, he'd decided to get some paperwork done. Brody was glad now that he'd come to his office.

He had what he wanted to say to Jake all written out. There were a few points that he'd wanted brought out if he took his case, as well as some questions that he had about the practice there, should he take it. Brody had been losing patients for a couple of weeks now. Nothing to do with him, but there was a large corporation that had come to down, and they were offering free office visits for six months if they signed on with them for a year. In six months—less, he thought—people would be pounding down his door. That was, if he was still there.

The knock at his door had him looking up. It was his nurse, telling him that there was a call for him on line two. He picked it up, thinking that it was going to be his mom. Instead, it was the police. There had been a death. Mrs. Mabel Little had laid down and hadn't woken again.

"I'm truly sorry, Brody. But she showed the nurse where she could find things, laid down on her little bed, and just let go. Poor old thing. Milly said that she'd been by to see you this morning. I'm so sorry. I know that you and Mrs. Little were really close." He rubbed his heart, thinking it would never be the same again without her around. "I'm to tell you that all the arrangements are made for her funeral. Told Milly that she, and I quote, 'ain't got nobody but that handsome doc, so the only people you call if I was to die is the cops, and they'll take care of the rest.'"

"That sounds like her."

They laughed at some of the things that she'd say to them, and when he hung up, he felt like all the goodness in the world had gone right on with her. Brody didn't know why, but he thought that she'd known that she wasn't long for this world. Closing up the office, he told the nurse he was going home, and drove there with a heavy heart. But as soon as he came into his home, he felt lighter than ever. Jordan and his mom were there.

~*~

Cam had dug up several things that he'd seen in his dreams by the time Jake and Forrest came out to see him. He'd not realized that it had gotten so late and was embarrassed to be caught digging up another man's land.

"I'm sure that he won't care. What is all this?" Cam was very proud of the glass jars that he'd found. Amazingly, not a one of them was rusted through. The seals on the top of most of them were made of paraffin over the top so that nothing could get in, he supposed. Handing the first one to Jake, he just looked at him. "You didn't open them? I wouldn't have been able to go digging anymore without seeing what I was working with."

"They're not mine." Cam smiled at them. "I wanted to, don't get me wrong, but going through them just didn't feel right, I guess. I was going to get them gathered up and take them in the house after I got this one up."

They worked for another ten minutes before he was able to unearth the last item that he'd seen. As he was telling them what he'd seen in his dreams, Cam laughed with them.

"I've never dreamed about things like this before. It's almost as if my dreams were invaded, and I was told that I needed to get these out of the ground." He handed him the little wooden box that he'd found just where he'd been told, among the other things in the barn. "You'll see that it's a Bible that's older than most people I know put together."

"A Bible. This is fantastic." Cam told them that it had been the Negro's Bible, as the person who had insisted that he find it had called it. "I've never had an occasion to use that word, so I'm sorry if I offended you."

"No, no you didn't. But this is fantastic, Cam." They gently thumbed through it, careful of the fragile pages and the binding. "We were told that there was a slave cemetery back there somewhere. I'm so glad that you've found it."

"It sort of found me, I'm afraid. As I was searching for things—like I said, like I was drawn to them—I had to go out there once and have a look around. I discovered one of the markers with the name Doolittle on it. I haven't a clue why that was important, but I know where it is now."

Putting all the items in one of the empty crates, they carried it into the house where Paddy and Rick were working. After

141

showing them what he'd found, telling them how he'd come to find them, Cam sat down with the others to open a couple of them. While they were working on the best way to get them open without damaging the things inside, Jake told them about his friend, Brody.

"He said that he had lost a patient, or he might have called me earlier in the day. I guess this woman was over a hundred, and he's mourning her loss. Brody is a good doctor, and a few months ago I called to ask him to come out for a visit and to help us run the clinic that Forrest and I are getting started." Cam asked him if he was coming. "Yes. He has a son, Jordan— he's about five—and Brody's mother will be joining them. He's in the process of getting his divorce taken care of. That was the real reason that he called—he needs a divorce lawyer. Forrest is going to do it for him."

Cam had, like the rest of them, heard about Jake's ex-wife, what a terrible and violent woman she'd been, as well as how she'd had the worst taste in furniture and clothing as anyone had ever seen. Cam had thought he was joking about how awful it was until Jake had shown him a picture taken of her one year.

The first jar that they opened was the one that had been out under an apple tree that had long since been killed by the frost. Opening it up, trying their best to guess what was in it before it had been opened, had them laughing. It was odd the things that one would think of as a treasure. As soon as it was dumped on the table, all they could do was stare at it.

"There must be seven-thousand dollars there." Jake picked it up and nodded. "At least. It isn't a great deal of money, not by today's standards, but by the numbers on the bills, I'd say that this is about ninety years old. Whoever saved that, they were either wealthy or had saved for their entire lifetime." Cam touched the tall stack of bills and shook his head. "What did you find out?"

"Train robbery." They asked if he was serious. "There isn't any more of it. The fellow, Kenneth Bruce, gave that to his mother, telling her that she needed to get herself and his sister away from there. Four days later Kenny, as his mom called him, was caught and hanged. She buried the money so that no one would come and take her to the gallows as well. The little sister, Mary, died the following winter."

"Well that's not a cheerful story." Cam told Jake he was sorry, but that was the truth of it. "I don't know what we'll do with it right now, but we'll do something good with it."

The next two jars were also money, but nothing close to what had been in the first one — a few silver coins, some copper plugs, as well as a holder's deed to a ranch out west. The latter was just what it sounded like — whoever held it, owned it.

Paddy said that he'd look into it in the morning. Cam knew that the land had never been claimed again, and now had people living there that had no real home or deed. It was Henry and Paddy's, so long as they could show this as proof, and he had a feeling that they'd be doing something good with it as well.

The last one that he'd found was the one that had been buried on the grave of a man by the name of Doolittle. It was the one that they'd been told about from the mother of the two boys that had died in the service. The men, Howie and Grant, appeared in the room with them when Paddy called for them. They looked like they were excited to see what their mother had left them. As soon as it was opened, the boys, they could see, were visibly upset.

In the old can was a cameo that Howie said that he'd gotten for his momma when he was about five or so. There was ninety cents in coin too, all of it silver, and the watch that belonged to Hamilton, their father, which Grant said hadn't worked for years before he'd gone off to war. There were also letters, one for each of them.

Since neither of them could read, they just held the papers in their hands, holding them close to their hearts. Cam hadn't been sure that a ghost could cry, but these men did. Large tears that dried as soon as they rolled down their cheeks. Jake asked them if they wanted them read to them.

"Not just yet, sir. We — I mean me — I'd like to just keep hold of it for a while." Grant nodded, as if that was his plan as well. "She didn't spell well, and her writing was terrible, but she put something to paper for us, and I want to just remember her for a little while whilst it's still fresh to me."

The envelopes were worn through and there were marks on them, like something had been pressed against them. Inside, without taking out the letters, they each found some petals. They had been a part of the lilac bush that had been in front of the home when they'd been living there.

Howie held the long dried out petals to his nose and sobbed like a child. It wasn't until Christy came into the room that he left. Grant said it wasn't proper for a man to bawl like a baby in front of a pretty lady. A few minutes later, Grant left them as well.

There was still one more jar to open and the Bible to go over. But they decided to have dinner first, just a light one of sandwiches and salad. When Grant returned, telling them that Howie was with Mom's stone, he sat with them to tell them about his life. Things that he'd not shared with Paddy and Rick yet.

"We was just barely boys when my daddy decided that he'd go and see about going to where they were working on the big buildings downtown. His job was to keep the others from being thirsty. They were darkies doing the heavy work, and nobody but my daddy would go near them; afeared of catching something, I suppose." He looked at the petals, all of them no more than dust by now, as he continued. "One afternoon, this here woman comes into town to see one of the men. The darkies. She told them that this one had to go home, his momma was passing, and she wanted him there."

No one said a word for several minutes. All sorts of things were going through his mind, none of them very good. When Grant started in on his story again, no one moved, not even Jenna, with her bottle hanging out of her mouth like she was waiting for the bad news.

"My daddy was a good man. Not strong—he'd been sickly all winter, and the doctor had told him that he'd be lucky if he made it through another one. But that woman, she was a crying and a sobbing, telling them that this man had to go. It was his momma's dying wish. So, my daddy, he takes the big hammer away from the man and tells him to go on home, that he'd do his job for him."

The silence was loud in the room. The big grandfather clock was ticking slowly, the heavy arm of it the only noise in the otherwise quietness of the house. Grant looked around the table, his face a mirror of pain while he finished up.

"My daddy worked all that day and into the next for the man. He comed home for supper that night and was barely moving, his body so messed up from working so hard that he couldn't even eat. So, he goes on to bed, leaving us all to wonder if Daddy thought working for the darkie had been too much. When the darkie came back to work the next afternoon, his momma passing with him there, he thanked my daddy for helping him out, saying that he'd do anything for him should he need it. Two days later, my own daddy went to bed that night and he didn't wake up. His poor old heart, the doctor told my momma, had plumb wore out."

Jenna puckered her lower lip; she looked as saddened by the story as the rest of them had been.

"What happened to the darkie, Grant?" The ghost looked at him, then asked him what he meant. "The man pledged himself to your family. Did he help out?"

"Yes, sir. Not just the man, but his whole family. They brunged over some of the best tasting vittles we'd had in a long while. A ham, too, that the man had butchered last fall. Hung it in the house so nothing could get to it." Grant smiled. "His sister, the one that comed to get him when his momma passed, she made sure that every day she and one of the other sisters comed by to help my momma with the garden and the yard. We had a garden, but it weren't nothing much to speak of, but them ladies, they had us plum tomaters to can, some apples from the trees out yonder. There was even meat on the table more'n twice a week, too. That man and his family, they not just saved our lives, but they took care of us for years and years after. And when my momma died, I heard tell that they even come to the house, wrapped her up all pretty, and put her in the ground for us. They didn't know we was both dead, they told me."

"Was his name Doolittle?" Grant nodded at him, his smile as big as Wally's was all the time. "Did you know that your momma put that tin can with the letters in it on his grave? That's where we found it. Sitting right there just under the soil, waiting for you both to come home."

"Well, ain't that plumb nice. He was a good man. His family helped mine well beyond the point of my daddy helping him out. 'Course, he lost his life, and maybe that's what they was thinking, I don't rightly know. I just remember having meat on the table and vittles when suppertime rolled around." Grant looked at his letter, then around the table at all of them. "I don't know that I want you to ever read my momma's words to me. She was the best there was, my momma, and her words, they might be private. She wouldn't have said too many things, her thinking that I'd learn to read in the service. But she took all that time to put words to paper, and I want to just hold onto them forever. You might have to read Howie's, but not mine. This here book that we're working on, maybe you can not put in there about my daddy. People don't seem no different about darkies now than they were back then. And I want you to have a good sale of it. You gonna charge much? I paid five cents for one once. It had the prettiest pictures in it."

After they gathered up to leave, Cam walked out to the cemetery where Doolittle was buried. Tomorrow, if no one objected, he was going to have it cleaned up out here and do some of the work all by himself. Yes, this was just what he needed to do, to keep himself busy while learning his job.

Chapter 11

Rachel hated Brody and his mother. Christ, she was the nosiest woman she'd ever encountered, and Brody was just like her. Like it was any of either of their businesses if she'd filed or not today. She'd been busy getting the new house ready. It was a good thing that she'd been stashing money all year. Now she not only had enough to get her a new home, but once Brody started paying for his kid, then she'd be set. Ralph was going to help out too when he could until he was able to divorce his wife and come stay with her.

Pulling out her key, she noticed that there was a strange car in the driveway. Not that it mattered to her — Brody was forever having someone over for this or that. And just last week, he'd informed her that he was having the pool dug. Who the fuck dug a pool in the middle of winter? Her husband might be a doctor, but he was a moron too.

"Mrs. Downs?" She nodded at the handsome man that had appeared out of nowhere. "My name is Jake Stout. I've been employed by Brody Downs. Here you go."

The envelope was shoved at her so quickly that she'd had

no choice but to take it. She didn't have time to be solicited by every Tom, Dick, and Virgil, so she put her key in the door and tried to get it to turn. The man who had given her the envelope was still there, leaning against the car, laughing.

"You know, the very least you could do is help me out here. I haven't any idea what you're trying to sell, but as you can see, I've literally got my hands full." Laughing again, he didn't bother moving, but told her that her key wouldn't work. "No shit, dumbass. Are you related to my husband? That sounds just like something that he'd say. 'Your key doesn't work. Try it again.'" She tried to sound like Brody, but all she managed was to sound like she had a terrible cold.

"It won't matter how many times you try it, it's not going to work. I advised him this morning to have the locks changed." Rachel stared at him. "In the event you haven't realized it, your husband has had you served. You are no longer welcome in his home. You have no access to his bank accounts or his credit cards, and the car that you've been driving is being repossessed."

Rachel looked out on the street, where she'd only just noticed that her car was gone. Glancing back at the man, who seemed to be having just too much fun at her expense, she asked him what she was supposed to use now, and how was she going to get her things from the house.

"You won't. None of it belongs to you, since you've never had a job since you've been married. The items that you've purchased today have been put back, and the house that you tried to buy this afternoon is also no longer an option for you." He grinned. If she wasn't so afraid he'd hit her back, she'd gladly hit him in the nose. "And since you've not asked, your son is now in the custody of the state, pending a blood test to see if he's the biological child of Brody Downs."

"Why the hell is he doing that? Christ, we've been married for ten damned years. It's his fucking kid." She thought that she remembered him saying his name was Jack or something. "Listen, Jack. I've thought it over, and I've decided to see a counselor for us. He can just stop this madness right now."

"Too late, and the name is Jake, not Jack. You must have me confused with one of the several men that you've been fucking in this house. You should really have a look around the rooms when you have guests over. There have been cameras in this house for months now."

No way. Brody wasn't that devious. Stomping toward Jake, she stopped when he stood up. The man seemed to grow about a foot. And not only that, but Rachel was sure that she could see fangs. Long sharp ones that seemed to be as sharp as any knife that she'd ever used. She paused again on the steps leading down to him when he laughed again.

"Where is he?" Jake asked her who. "My husband, you fucking bastard. I want to talk to him right now. And I want him to stop those tests on my son. I did not give him authorization to hurt him, and he'll not do it or I'll sue."

"Good luck with that. And while Ohio isn't a divorce fault state, he will still not only win custody of Jordan, but he'll take you to the cleaners while he's at it." Jake got into his car and rolled down the window as she stood there.

Rachel was afraid. She was in deeper shit than she'd thought. All her money was in that house, stashed in all her things that she'd been planning to take out of there today while Brody was at work. But that had gotten waylaid when she'd met Jon for an afternoon at the hotel, then Ralph had said that he'd found them a house. Christ, she wasn't sure what to do or where to go.

Rachel stopped the man before he left her. "I need some

cash. Surely, he doesn't mean for me to be without a place to stay until we can work things out. You give me a couple of hundred bucks, and you can get it back from Brody." She gave him her best smile. "Or, you and I can fuck each other against this prime car, and we'll call it even. What do you think of that?"

"I'd rather you cut my dick off and use it for a flag pole. You are just one nasty bitch," he answered, revving the engine while staring at her. Rachel unbuttoned her blouse as she took the necessary steps to reach him. "Not on your life, lady. As I said, I'm not going to touch you. You've been with more men than the entire population of homosexual men that I know. And lady, that is a good many men."

"Men? Oh my God. You're gay? Why are all the good-looking ones gay?" She grinned at him, knowing that men sometimes said shit like that when they were married or something. "How about we get it on, buddy? I have no doubt that you're as big as the flagpole that you compared yourself to earlier. Come on. What could it hurt?"

"You've been served, Rachel Downs, and your court date is in two days. I really hope you don't show up. It would be wonderful to be able to wonder who you're fucking today."

When he pulled out of the drive, her drive, she screamed and stomped her foot.

It took her ten minutes to get back to town, but she'd broken one of her heels, got a run in both legs of her pantyhose, and discovered that her cell phone was no longer working. That fucking prick had already turned it off. And the worse part of that was she didn't have a clue what anyone's phone numbers were to call for help.

By the time she made it to the library to use their phone, the place had closed down. This wasn't going to bode well for Brody once she got to talk to him. The little shitter was going to pay for all this crap. And the fact that he'd beaten her to the draw meant that she'd have to find her own attorney. When she remembered Jake, or whatever his name was, she realized that she could use the family attorney. Things suddenly were looking up for her.

It was dark by the time she had convinced the hotel to let her stay one night. Her mother, who she'd been trying to get ahold of for two hours, wasn't answering her phone. And she knew that her dad was once again in county lock up. When she was able to remember the family attorney's name, it was too late to call his office. Rachel had no choice—she was going to have to stay here and wait until morning.

Finally getting in touch with her mom about ten o'clock, she told her what Brody had done to her. Her mother told her that she'd been informed of it as well. Rachel asked her mom why she'd been informed, when Rachel still didn't know what the hell was going on.

"Well, he wants us out of his house." Rachel must have missed the stupid people bus, thank God, and told her mom that she didn't live with them. "No, but he does own the house what we're in. Your father and I have twenty-four hours to get out of the house, and if we do any damage to it, take anything other than the clothing on our backs, when the police come to take us out, then he will sue us for whatever we do. Christ, Rachel, what the hell did you do to piss him off? I told you that he was much smarter than you gave him credit for. And now, after living here for ten years, having everything that we've ever wanted done to the house, we're being kicked out because you couldn't keep your husband happy and in the dark about what you were doing. You did this to us."

"What am I supposed to do now? He's locked me out of my home, and I haven't any way of getting anything out of it.

153

I had money there." She told her that she should have thought of those things before she spouted off about getting a divorce. "You're blaming this on me? I had nothing at all to do with him growing a set of balls and doing something before me. Christ, Mom, I've had to do everything for him since we've been married."

"Like what, Rachel? The only thing that I've ever seen you do is for yourself. Your husband—your soon-to-be-ex-husband—has been doing it all throughout your relationship, including getting up with Jordan." Her mom laughed; it was bitter sounding to Rachel. "Have you thought of what you're going to do when he finds out that Jordan isn't his? You might as well kiss any kind of support out the fucking window. He's not going to pay you shit, and you were stupid enough to sign that paper when we both, your father and I told you not to."

"Had I not signed it when he offered to put you into a home so long as we were married, then your ass would be in the poor house, along with Daddy's. Will you fucking stop blaming everything on me and help me out? I need money." Her mother laughed again. All this was getting on her last nerve. "Now what the fuck is so funny? Just sneak something out—we'll split whatever we can get for it. Hopefully it's enough to me something to wear. I've had these clothes on all day. And I stink."

"I can't take anything from the house, I've told you that." So she had, but Rachel asked her if she could try. "No. And I will especially not try and take something for you to have an outfit. Have you always been this selfish, Rachel? Oh wait, I know the answer to that—yes, you have. I want you to—"

The line went dead, and she tried to call her mom back. But the line, this mechanical voice told her it had been disconnected and if they wanted to resume service to call the office. Putting

154

the phone down, she let out a long breath, then another one, trying to calm herself before she did damage to the room. If she did, Rachel would go to jail, if she didn't already have to because her mom had no money either. This was a shitstorm, and all because Brody had gotten a bug up his ass.

Pulling out the stationery that she would normally have tossed in the trash, Rachel started making notes on what she wanted to say to Brody. He'd better not have had Jordan tested, that's all she had to say about that. Then she started a note of things that she wanted from the house. She knew that she couldn't just ask for her money—he'd take that—but Rachel had to remember where she'd put it so that she could ask for those items. This was a nightmare.

Rachel had never liked the house. It had been his before he married her, and she'd never been able to make him sell it to get something for her. He wouldn't even talk about it. Brody would update it when it needed it. The kitchen had been done every other year since she'd moved in, and that was okayed by the cook.

The only place that Rachel could have fun was in her office. But there was a limit on how much she was allowed to spend on it, too. And that was as boring as fuck. Four walls, one window that she could look out, and nothing more. There wasn't even a decent fireplace in the room for her to snuggle up with her lovers in front of.

Taking off her clothing, she took a quick shower—not getting her hair wet because she didn't have anything to fix it back to its glorious fullness—then went to bed. She wasn't the least bit comfortable, nor was she very happy. She did wonder for a moment if Brody was aware of how difficult he was making everyone's life and knew that he was.

"This is just like him to do something like this and not let me win. He was forever the one that came out on top." She thought about it another moment. "Because he has all the money, and he flipping knows it. Damn him. Well, he's not going to win this time. I'm going to get Jordan from him, and hold him over his head forever."

Could she do that? The test was sure to come back that Jordan wasn't his son. He didn't even look like Brody, not even a little bit. And once he found out, no fault state or not, he'd never pay her anything to raise him. That brought up the question, did she want to keep Jordan if Brody didn't give her support? No. She knew the answer to that even before the question settled in her mind. But she'd never let Brody know that. She could be just as cruel and uncaring as he could.

~*~

Cattie hated missing a day of running. She could have, she supposed, used the equipment in the basement that Cam had put in, but she wanted the outdoors, the fresh air, and the color of fall. It was still cold and wet, but she needed this more than she could have explained to anyone.

Stretching, she noticed the man with the stroller coming toward her. Cattie didn't bother telling him that it was a private track. Perhaps he was a friend of one of them. Since she didn't care, she resumed what she was doing.

"Good morning. I don't think I've seen you on this path before." She just shook her head at him. "I'm babysitting my nephew."

"That's good." Finishing up, she made her way to the track. The man laughed when she stretched her foot out. A little bit of a cramp made her a little nervous about how long it had been since she'd run. The man asked her if she was all right. "Yes. I'm just fine."

Running now, she felt better. Her muscles protested a bit—

they were as tight as she'd ever allowed them to be. And when she let go of her aggravation of the man interrupting her time, she could see that this was a perfect day to do this.

The sound of running feet annoyed her again, but she closed off her mind to everything but her feet hitting the pavement. She was going to tell her brother when she got back that there were others using his property, and she wanted him to do something about it. It wasn't like she couldn't take care of herself. She really could.

Cattie had her gun on her, as well as a knife. The knife would do her little good other than to cut through some rope. It wasn't long enough to stab someone and do any real damage, but the gun and both magazines would make someone pay attention to her when she said no or stop.

The ground came up fast after something hit her from behind. As soon as she knocked her head on the pavement, she felt blood splatter on her face. It disoriented her for several seconds, long enough for the big burly man to leap on her and try and tear at her clothing. Her shirt was ripped, the sound of it saying more than she wanted to admit, and then nothing. The man was gone, her shirt with him.

Cattie wasn't sure what had happened and sat up slowly. Her head was swimming, and her nose was bleeding pretty badly by now. Holding onto her head, she tried to think beyond the pain as to what had happened. Did she trip?

"Are you all right?" The man, the one with the stroller, asked. He was handing her his shirt, which she gladly took. She was nearly naked and had forgotten about that. "Miss? Are you all right?"

"I hurt." He knelt down to her, and she could see the scratches on his face. Touching her fingers to them, Cattie looked at him. "Are you hurt?"

"Not really. Nothing a quick shift won't help." She asked about his baby, feeling the pain in her head as she tried to stand up. "I don't have a child, miss. I was...it was a ruse to look harmless, miss. Or to you, annoying."

"I didn't want to be bothered today." She watched him stand up and go to the fallen stroller. Taking out what looked like a first aid kit, he opened it beside her on the pavement. "Where did burly go?"

"The guy? He's gone." She didn't ask anything else. Cattie was sure that she didn't want to know. "I didn't expect anyone to be out here today. This is private property."

"My brother owns it." He grinned. It was so sexy that she felt her heartrate go up a couple of notches. "You're not as charming as you might think you are. And you were trespassing. My brother won't care for that."

"I just saved your pretty little ass for you, and you're giving me grief? You're very charming, in a bitchy sort of way. I think that you're going to need a few stitches. Unless you can shift." She said that she wasn't a shifter. "You smell like...cat, bear, and wolf. I guess I thought you were one of those."

When he leaned in and sniffed her neck, Cattie moaned. She didn't even try to stop it. And when the stranger licked her throat, she grabbed him on the back of the head, intending, she told herself, to push him away. But he bit down on her and Cattie came.

"You're too beautiful to let someone hurt you, did you know that?" He lowered her to the ground, her head touching the pavement gently. And when he kissed her, plundering her mouth like he was searching for treasures, Cattie felt her brother touch her mind. It was all she needed to bring her back to where she shouldn't be.

He sat up with her when she pushed him away. Cam asked

her if she was all right, and she told him to meet her at the hospital. That she'd fallen. Cattie could take his laughter right now—it would be better than him being pissed off about the man. She looked at him now.

"My brother is going to meet me at the hospital." He nodded but didn't move. "I should get going. I don't know why you were here, but you should—"

"You know what you are to me." Cattie shook her head. "Mate. You're my mate. I'm Tyson Huffman. You're...I'm assuming that your last name is Henderson, if Cam is your brother."

"He is." She didn't tell him her first name, not sure she wanted him to know just now. "I have to go to the hospital. You said that I might need stitches."

"If you let me lick it clean, then you and I will have a connection, as well as you'll be healed." She stood up. "Yeah, for some reason I didn't think you'd let me."

When she stood there for several seconds, she felt the earth move under her feet. Like in a romantic way, but more. Like— holy shit, it was an earthquake. Reaching out to grab onto anything close, she felt her hands curve around taut muscle, then there was nothing else.

Cattie woke up in a moving car. Her head was pounding, and she felt sick. When she looked over at the driver, thinking that it would be Cam, she had to think what the man's name was.

"Tyson. You fainted, and I realized that you might have concussed yourself. I've contacted Cam, and he's on his way to the hospital." She started to nod but decided that if she did that again, she would be puking all over herself. "I could have healed you while you were out, but I didn't want you not to trust me. I'm telling you that now so that you know that I can

159

be trusted, with no meaning no."

"I think I'm going to be sick." He pulled over immediately and hopped out of the car. He was coming around to her side of it when she felt like she wasn't going to make it. Leaning over when Tyson had the door open, it was all she could do not to puke on his shoes. But he didn't seem to mind. Cattie had never had anyone hold her hair back for her when she was sick.

"All right now, lean back, and I'm going to buckle you in again." She'd not even realized that she'd been unbuckled. Tyson was so gentle with her that she nearly sobbed. It wasn't like her to be so emotional, but Cattie felt that she deserved a little self-pity after the morning she'd had already. "Okay, here is my other shirt. I've got a pair of pants back there too. They'll be a little big, but you can pull them on over yours if you want. I'm afraid that yours have seen better days."

"I just got these." She bemoaned the fact that she'd torn her pants but didn't care that he was seeing a good portion of her leg and thigh. "I don't feel so well."

"I know, honey. I'm getting you help. I'm glad now that I didn't seal up the wound. You could have been really sick if I'd done that. You must be brilliant for not allowing me to help you." She looked at him. "Well, it's better than thinking that you didn't want me touching you, don't you agree?"

It was the wink that got her. He really was charming and sweet. And he was taking such good care of her, she could have just rolled over into his body and stayed there. She needed to tell him some things about her, things that would more than likely turn him off her. But she was just too sick and in too much pain to bother.

Cattie must have blacked out again, because the next time she woke she was getting her head x-rayed. Tyson was with her again, holding her hand while she laid there. When they told her that she could move, Cattie looked at him. Tears filled her eyes when she saw the worried look on his face.

"Don't cry, baby. It's going to be just fine." She told him she was sorry. "For what? You helped bring down a bad guy. You got to meet me, and we get to tell our children about this someday when we're old and gray."

"I'm not human." She whispered that to him, knowing that as a wolf he'd hear her. When he leaned down and kissed her on the mouth, he told her that he wasn't either. "Yes, but you don't understand. I'm not just not human, I'm like Cam."

"He told me."

They were taken to a room, and Cam and Rick were there. She was asked a million questions, all of which Tyson answered. He told them about the attempt on her life, leaving out the attempted rape. Also, how she'd hit her head and how she was going to be fine. Right now, she didn't feel fine at all.

The doctor came in sometime later. She was given something for pain, and then her head was stitched up. Forty-four stitches, and she had a nasty — his words, not hers — concussion. Closing her eyes, Cattie let the drugs take her away, and the entire time, Tyson held her hand.

Waking up, the room was dark and there was something heavy next to her. Crying out, pushing as best she could, Cattie calmed down when she heard Tyson's voice in the darkness. At some point he had gotten in the bed with her. Cattie thought that was the best medicine she'd ever had. She laid there, letting his hand stroke her shoulder while he spoke.

"I thought for sure that I'd have your name by now. I didn't ask anyone, nor did I have a peek at your arm bracelet. Not a very pretty one, by the way. Anyway, you're going to be just fine, my dear. I know that you can take care of yourself, and I'm happy to know that, but I'd like, once in a while, if you'd allow me to be manly with you." She looked up at him, telling him her name. "Caitlynn. That's very pretty. Do they call you that or Cait?"

"Cattie." He nodded; she could see him now. "Cam and I are twins, and when he was given something after a bad accident, somehow I got it too. When I say that I'm not human, I want you to know that I don't really know what you'd call me."

"Lovely comes to mind. Beautiful. Intelligent. Mine. That last part is something that I wanted to talk to you about." She nodded but laid her head on his chest. "Yes, well, this is too nice to make you move. We'll talk when you feel better. And Caitlynn, I'm already in love with you. I wanted you to know that right away."

"I love you too." He lifted her chin up, careful not to do it too fast. "I don't know when that happened. It could be just that I'm emotionally distraught right now, but I'm pretty sure that I love you."

"I'll take it." He kissed her on the mouth, just a simple kiss that warmed her to her toes. And when she snuggled closer to him, he laughed. "I wish this bed were a tad bigger and you were in less pain. I'd show you just how much I need you."

"I need you too. Now, shut up. I'm exhausted, and I need my rest."

When he laughed, she smiled. This might not be so bad, having someone in her life like this. Hearing his heart beating, the steadiness of it like a lullaby that she'd heard as a child, Cattie fell into a deep sleep.

Chapter 12

Rick was bored out of his mind. He laughed at that thought since he'd never had that sort of feeling before. Usually, before finding Cam, it'd been because he was broke all the time. Now, it was because he had nothing to do.

The book that he and Paddy were working on was coming along nicely. In a few more weeks, less he'd bet, the man would be sending it to be sold on the market. It really was going to be a hit, Rick thought. There was a little of everything in it—sex, intrigue, as well as romance and true love. All of it being true would make people want more. And with all the ghosts that were around his and Cam's house, there would be plenty of stories for him to tell too.

Opening his email, he looked twice at the number of them. Four hundred since last night? He opened the first one, the last one he'd received, and it was from an author that he'd known before the scandal. Reading the first few lines, Rick laughed. He needed him to edit his book and wondered if he was taking on new authors.

The rest were about the same. A few needed to know if he

was opening his own publishing company. Others wanted to know what he charged to get a book on the market, and he even had a few that wanted to know what the name of his company was so that they could feature it on their website. He sat there for several seconds, thinking about what was going on. Then he yelled for Wally.

"Did you do this? Put the word out that I'm opening a company?" The man smiled. "I see. I don't suppose that it occurred to you to ask me about it first?"

"Oh, sure, it occurred to me, but then I figured you'd just tell me no, so I talked it over with Jenna and she said to do it. You needed something to do." He did but didn't tell Wally that. "You've been a moping around this house for four days, sir. And I think you need to get your bottom in gear."

"I don't have a company, nor do I know what to charge should I have one. And I'm reasonably sure that it's a lot more complicated than just getting a few emails answered so that I can work." Wally laughed, and said that if anyone could do it, he could. "Yes, I'm sure that you'd think that. Or did Jenna tell you to tell me that?"

"Miss Jenna. She said that if you ask the right people, you can have a business set up in no time. And the money is good. I don't know what that would be to you, but even if'n you only make a dollar a book, it's more'n you're making right now." That was true. "Besides, you might find that you're really good at it. Jenna, she told me that there are all kinds of stuff on that there computer you seem so fond of that you can look up."

He was sure that was a jab at him, but he wasn't ready to ask him about it. While talking to Wally, three more emails popped up. Rick read the first few lines of each of them, and then another one came up. This one was from his old publishing company.

Hello, Richard. I was just looking over things on the Internet this morning and imagine my surprise when I saw that you were looking for clients. I was also a little hurt by your actions without coming to me first about this. You haven't the first clue as to what it takes to take on this venture, and I'm actually surprised that you, of all people, would think that you could make this work for you. Besides, I thought that you and I had a good working relationship – the one where you just wrote, and I took care of all the details on things. And if you don't count that little matter of the man falsely accusing you of plagiarizing your book, I'd say that we both made some good money, too.

It hadn't seemed like a little matter to him when it happened, and Parker had dropped him quicker than the movie deal that he'd had. But Rick was intrigued, so he continued reading.

Right now, I have a runaway best seller in my stable, but I'm sure that I could make room for one more and would like to invite you to come back and work for us. I'm sure that you'd not mind changing your name – a pen name, as it were – and we'll start as if nothing had happened. I don't need you coming along and bringing the stigma of that other incident here with you, now do I? And, Richard, I don't have to tell you how difficult and expensive it is to self-publish. I'm sure that with your research, you've found that what I'm saying is true.

Let us let bygones be bygones, and work to make us both successful again. I look forward to hearing from you by the end of the day, and if you could send me a little peek at whatever it is you're working on, I'll see what I can do about getting some new covers made up for you. That, too, is an expensive endeavor, and you should more than likely leave that to the professionals. Your friend in writing, Stanley Parker of Parker Publishing.

The post script at the bottom had him laughing hard enough to bring Wilbur from the kitchen.

Oh, before I forget, if you'd be so kind as to stop advertising that you're looking for authors, I'll put out an ad in our published books magazine that you aren't taking anyone on and are working for us.

He laughed for a full ten minutes. The last line was what had him thinking that he could do this no matter what Stanley said about how expensive or hard it was. He wasn't a stupid man, and he could learn something as easily as the next person. Looking at the links that he found, after a couple of hours he knew that it was much easier than he'd thought but also more expensive than he'd realized.

By six-thirty, when Cam came home from work, not only did he have a list of potential clients, but he also had a draft of the letter that he was sending back to good old Stan. Rick had Cam read it over three times, after he'd read the one from Parker Publishing, to see if he'd been just nasty enough.

When Cam was finished, he leaned back in his chair. Rick was glad now that he'd not sent the letter. His lover was going to tell him that he thought this was a terrible idea, and that he should just back away now before it was too late. Standing up to tear up his list, Cam grabbed his hand to stay him.

"Today I had to fire an agent for shooting his wife in the foot when she wouldn't get him a beer. I asked him why he'd not gotten it himself, as she too had worked that day, and he said that he didn't know, but it seemed like she was egging him on by telling him what a day she'd had." Rick asked him what that meant. "I want you to think if you truly want to do this, because there is no doubt in my mind that you can. Or— and this is really important—are you doing this because he was egging you on? Either way, I'll support you in whatever you decide."

Rick began to pace. It wasn't something that he normally did, but he'd picked up the habit from living with Cam and Cattie, who did it all the time. He thought about what Cam had asked him. Really thought about it.

"When the first few emails that I read were so positive, I thought perhaps I could do this. Then as I gathered more emails and read them, I could see the possibility of making this work for a few people. They don't just want me to help them, Cam, but they want me to run a publishing company so that I can help them like I have Paddy." Cam asked him what he thought now. "Even before the email came from Stan, I was seriously thinking about calling you and asking if you had a place I could hang my name. I know that you have a couple of offices, and the one thing that I've learned from Stan is not to have a place of business at your home. He was either eating, talking to his children, or mowing instead of helping his stable, as he called them."

"I'm not sure that answered my question." Rick said that he was getting to it. "All right. And yes, we have plenty of space in the market district that you can use. Anyone of them that aren't earmarked for demo. Also, there are two that I think will be perfect. But go on."

Rick was sidetracked for a moment and had to rethink what he'd been saying.

"Oh, yes. Well, then I got the email from Stan and read it several times. I came to the conclusion that he was somewhat threatening me." Cam said that he was, in a small way. "Yes, well, I don't think I liked it, however he did it. And the email I was sending him back, that was sort of a stick-it-up-your-ass kind of thing that I should more than likely rethink."

Cam leaned forward on the desk, and then leaned back again with a grin that Rick was sure was bigger than Wally's. "I sent it. Just like it is. The man will either shit his pants in thinking that you've hit it big, or he'll send you another threatening letter—and then I'll take action. No one messes with my family."

Rick wanted to tell him that he'd made a mistake. Rick knew that he'd come to regret this. But really, right now, all he could think about was that he was going to open his own company. Cam was going on about staff and such, Internet in wherever he was going, as well as new computers, when Rick sat down hard and put his head between his knees. It was suddenly going too fast for him.

The hand at the back of his neck was comforting, but the laughter was not. When he tried to lift his head up to talk to Cam, he was pushed back down. He told him that he was all right now.

"I'm sure that you are, but I wanted to talk to you, and I'd rather I had your full attention and you're not pacing the room or worrying about emails. Tell me what you plan to do with this business. The reason that I ask you is because Cattie had decided that she'd like to try her hand at a romance. With sex, she told me." Rick raised his head and looked at Cam, asking him if he was serious. Cam nodded. "I'm not sure what I think about it. My first thought is, why not? I think she'd be good at it. Her vocabulary is certainly strong enough."

"Yes, there is that. But I don't know. I don't know if I could read it." Cam said that was going to be his issue as well. "I mean, you mentioned hiring a staff. Perhaps we can have one of them read it and do the work. But I'm sure that she can do it as well as anyone, don't you?"

"Yes. As I said, she has a strong vocabulary, and she's smart too." Cam laughed. "She might make it especially dirty just to shock us. I don't know if you're aware of this or not, but she had a nasty sense of humor."

"I've noticed." Rick missed the younger woman. "She's happy, you think? I mean, Tyson, he seems like a nice enough guy, and he sure has her best interest at heart. I've never seen her so — well, happy before."

"She comes home tomorrow. Tyson came over last night and told me that he has fallen in love with her, and that he'll take good care of her. I told him that if he didn't, he wouldn't have to worry about any of us. She was quite capable of kicking his ass better than us." Rick asked Cam what he said. "He agreed. Told me that he's already in love with her, and she thinks she is with him. Oh, and he's going to be working at the stationhouse with her. Tyson was hired by the Feds to come in and help her clean house. All I can think about is they'll get nothing done if they're anything like we are as mates."

"That's for sure." They were just sitting there when the computer signaled that there was an email. Neither one of them moved aside from Rick turning to Cam. "I just know that it's from Stan. He's going to be suing me or something, isn't he?"

"Not if I have anything to say about it. Oh, I have contacted Jake and Forrest. They're going to make sure that you have all your T's crossed and I's dotted. Jake said that you'd have to come up with a good name so that he can make sure that you're incorporated. That, he said, is the best way to go."

Turned out it was from Parker Publishing's attorney. Instead of reading it over, Rick forwarded it to Jake, and he told him that he'd gotten it. After only ten minutes, he called him back, laughing like a loon about something.

"I've taken care of this for you. Christ, the man is off his noodle. He said that he's going to sue you for breach of contract.

I know for a fact that he only had a one-year contact on you, and that it ran out thirty-six months ago. Also, and this is really funny, he said that you promised in a verbal conversation that the two of you had today that you wouldn't be opening your own company. By the way, I've given your company a name I made up quickly. Tell me if you have something else in mind and we'll get that filed for you today. Forrest said that he has a couple of connections at the county building, and he'll have it posted two days ago." Jake told him the name he'd come up with, and Rick loved it. "All right. We'll file it today, and by this time tomorrow, it will be all over the Internet that you've opened for business. Also, I've taken great pleasure in telling the world what Parker Publishing did to you. It's all true, by the way. And I think that you might have a case against them if you ever want to pursue it for misrepresentation with the man who lied about you."

Cam had left him when the phone had rung. He came back just as Rick was putting the finishing touches on the contract that Jake had sent him. He officially had representation, as well as a new name, which he ran by Cam when he sat down.

"Perfect. I like it. Simple, yet it says that you're ready to take on the world. I do love it. Yes, that'll look good on a sign outside your door." Cam grinned. "I just made us reservations to celebrate. How about we get dressed up, go to dinner, and have some fun later?"

He told him it sounded like a plan. As they were being driven to the restaurant, he thought of the new venture that he was taking one. World Castle Publishing was going to be huge. Rick couldn't wait to get it started.

~*~

Brody looked over the paperwork that had been delivered by courier. It was not just the divorce papers, but also a picture of Rachel accepting the paperwork that said that she'd been served. But there was also a nice video of her trying to get into the house, which Brody thought he'd cherish for a long time.

"You're really doing it?" He told his mom that he was. "Good for you. And I just heard from a friend of mine that works in social services. Jordan has been calling for you for the last hour."

"I got to talk to him. They let him call me. I told him that I would be picking him up in the morning. I can't believe how quickly that test came back." He felt his heart hurt. "He's not mine by blood, Mom. I won't give him up, but they just told me that there is a ninety-nine percent probability that he's not my son. They asked me what I wanted them to do with the information. I asked for it to be sent to my attorney. Jake Winslow. I won't give him up, Mom. Jake is this hot shot attorney. I can't wait to see him and the rest of his buddies. He was super nice before and seems to be still."

Mabel had died three days ago, and he'd been surprised to be named executor of her estate. Not only that, but the fact that she'd had everything taken care of—funeral arrangements, as well as her headstone picked out—and it was all taken care of well before she'd passed on. He was just telling his mom that he needed to get over to the funeral home and make sure that was paid for as well when his front door bell rang.

Letting the staff answer it, he was startled when Bentley came to tell him that he had something to sign for, a thick envelope from a firm called Winchester and Dodd. Taking it to his office after signing for it, he looked it over for anything that might harm him—he didn't trust Rachel about anything— when his mom handed him the letter opener and told him to get with it.

Brody read it four times before he was able to speak to his

mom. She asked him several times if he was all right, and all he could do was nod. Finally, she took it from him, and sat down as she read the first line of the letter that came with the last will and testament of Mabel Little. She had left him everything in her estate.

"I don't understand." Brody didn't either. When he was finished reading over the will, he leaned back in his chair and tried to think what had made her want to do that. "Didn't you tell me that she told you that she had no one left? I mean, it might not be that much."

Brody didn't say anything but handed his mom the last page of the paperwork that she'd dropped. It was a tally of all that she'd left him, and it was well over four million dollars in just cash alone. Mom set the paper down and went to the door to the hall.

"Bentley, we're going to need something throat burning to drink in here." Bentley pointed out that it was only just after ten. "Yes, I'm aware, but my baby boy just got the news of his life, and I think we could all use it. What a wonderful time to celebrate."

"Mom, you make it sound as if I needed this. I didn't. This is wonderful, as you said, but there are surely more deserving people out there than me." She shrugged and poured him a glass of bourbon. He took her glass, the one for Bentley, and his, pouring about a third of it in each of the other two. "I should do something with it. Help out some charity or something."

"You could use it to buy a new house and leave this one to me." He looked at his mom and then at Bentley, who was nodding with Mom. "You know as well as I do that Rachel isn't going to give up. I'll stay here, sell off the house and whatever else you don't want—which to me would be anything she sat her ass on. Then I'll follow you with Bentley here, if he wants to go."

"I do, as a matter of fact." Bentley was still recovering from snorting bourbon up his nose when his mom talked about furniture. "Your soon-to-be-ex-wife likes neither one of us, as you know. And, if we're not telling her where you've gone, even if it's only for a little while, she'll soon get the hint that you are finished with her."

He didn't believe that, and he doubted very much that either one of them did either. Rachel was a lot of things — cunt was his mom's favorite word to call her — but she wasn't one to give up. Nor was she, as much as everyone wanted to believe it, a nice or stupid person. She was a bitch and she was controlling. Things that he'd never noticed about her until the last few years or so. And she hated that he could control things better than her.

The more he thought of their plan, the better that he liked it. He'd be away from her, then when Mom had finished up here, they'd join him wherever he put his cap, and they'd use his house money to do something for Mrs. Little. He thought about the clinic/hospital that he was going to go help out at for a few months.

Brody realized that he was feeling much better about life in general. Not just because he'd finally gotten himself in gear and decided to divorce Rachel, but his life, up until now, had been basically on easy street. He needed things to spice up his life. Something to get his heartrate going once more. But he'd already decided that he would never marry again.

Jordan was coming home in the morning, and he told his mom that he was going to make arrangements now to take him on a trip. After this, it would be good for the two of them to get away. She asked him if he was going to tell him that he wasn't his father.

"I don't know. I will tell him—I believe he has a right to know. But the timing could be better, I think. I don't want him to think that him not being my son is why I'm leaving his mom." Mom told him that she was pretty sure that Jordan had heard them fighting. "I'm sure that he has. Rachel can be very loud when she thinks that she's right. Even if I've proven her wrong."

In less than two hours he had called Forrest to ask if it was all right to bring Jordan with him, and to ask him about the results of the testing. Forrest told him that Jake had been looking for a house for him, and a staff. This wasn't moving too fast, he'd just decided, but just about perfect for the four of them. Bentley and Mom would love being all set up like this.

"He's not your biological son, no, but what do you feel about being his father? Any changes there?" Brody didn't even have to think about it—he told him that he was his father first and foremost. "Good. I want you to make sure that you treat him the same as you would have before. I'm to understand that you've had him tested before?"

"Yes, but no one knows but me and now you." Forrest asked if he'd done the test himself. "I did. I was sure that he wasn't when he was born, but that didn't matter after I laid eyes on him. He was my son, no matter what the tests said."

"That'll show that you're not only going to be a more stable parent for him, but a loving one as well. I'm going to mention that test, only in passing, to your soon-to-be-ex-wife's attorney, and tell him that even though you knew then, you've never once treated him any differently than anyone would their own child. Also, that the wife lied to you from the start. I have a copy of the birth certificate now. She filled it out and put your name on it. That shows that she's a liar. Oh, I talked to your mom. Christ, she's a hoot."

"I'll have to tell her you said that. She and my butler and longtime friend, Bentley, are going to stay here in the house while I'm there. I read the note from you about that being just what it is, a helping out from one friend to another. Can you tell me why?" Forrest explained. "Oh. But the house even isn't in her name, and it never was. Can she still get me for abandonment?"

"We just don't want to take any chances on this." Now that, he understood. "I'm making arrangements for you to live in a hotel until this matter of finding you a house is taken care of. We're going to put it down that a hotel is no place to have a child, and that you're only renting. If you approve of the house, we'll buy it, then 'rent' it to you. That way, nothing is out of order."

It seemed to him like a lot of things were being done under the table. But then, Rachel had been doing that to him for years. Nothing from her was on the up and up. As he packed up some things for his son to take, he picked up his book, the one that a family would fill out for firsts—first day home, first steps, things like that.

Opening it to the first page, he looked at the ultrasound photo that he himself had put in the book. As he thumbed through the book, just smiling at the things that had been filled out, all by him, he watched his little boy simply grow up right before his eyes. Then at the back, he found a copy of Jordan's birth certificate, the one that he'd not been able to find earlier.

When it fell to the floor it landed on the face, and Brody picked it up to read the names on the back that were in Rachel's handwriting. He called Jake. This was terrifying to say the least.

"I'm sorry to keep bugging you, but I found something just now. It was in my son's baby book." He read off the six names there. "At the top of it she's written 'potential fathers of this brat.' None of them are my name."

"I'm sorry." Brody had to wipe the tears away. He'd known that Jordan wasn't his—even proved it twice over now. But to see names that weren't his listed that could be Jordan's father, in her handwriting, hurt him to the very core. "I'll get on this right away. Please don't say anything to your mom. I have a feeling that she'd be hunting down these men to let them know. But I'll take care of it. You trust me, don't you?"

"I do." He looked at the ultrasound picture again and touched his finger over the little bean looking person there. "I'm truly not his father, and she knew it."

Jake said again that he was sorry and would take care of it. Brody couldn't speak, not even to tell him that he would bring it with him. Putting his phone away, he finished the task of packing up for Jordan, then sat down on his bed. So much... there was just so much going on to change both of their lives, and Brody could only hope that it was going to end up with the two of them still father and son.

Chapter 13

William Henderson picked up the chair that had been offered for him to sit and talk to his son. What a major disappointment he'd been, from birth until now. But, he'd promised Cameron that he'd go and talk to him, to see if he could figure out what Cam's father had been thinking.

If anyone was to ask William, he'd tell them that Orval hadn't been thinking since the day he was born. And when he did venture to think, it was usually something about him, and how if it didn't benefit him at all, he was no longer interested. Moron.

The hallway wasn't that long, but he could see which cell was Orval's, even before he was halfway down the hall. There was paper laying right outside it, a tray that Willy could only assume was his breakfast tray — it was only ten in the morning — and a pile of clothing. Willy wondered if the moron thought that there was laundry service or something. It would be just like him.

When he stood up, Willy looked to see if he'd been mistaken, that this wasn't his son's cell. But as soon as he opened his mouth to complain about him being there, he knew it was him. Sitting down on the chair, he just shook his head at the mess in front of him. Not just the cell, but his son.

"What do you want? If you need money, Cameron has it all. And his sister. And they won't share it." Willy asked him why he thought they should share something they'd worked for. "They no more worked for it than you did. It just fell into your laps, like you were some sort of gods or something."

"No, that's not even close to how that works. We've worked hard for what we have. And not sharing with you? Well, that's a given. You're a greedy little shit that doesn't deserve to have those wonderful children." He asked him who told him that. "Everyone that meets you. Even those that have only heard of you. You have a reputation for being the person not to go to for good advice or friendship. I wasn't even in this town for an hour, and I heard of three things that you've done to mess up Cameron and Caitlynn's lives. What is wrong with you?"

"Nothing that a few hundred thousand dollars won't fix. When are you going to die, old man? I know you have everything all fixed up in your will. Your arrangements are made, so I don't have to bother with that. If you were to keel over, you'd make me a very happy man." Willy said that he wasn't planning on dying for a while now. "How the hell old are you? Seventy? Eighty? Well past a time that you should be pushing up daisies, as they say."

"I'm seventy-four. Thanks so much for keeping up with that. And let me tell you something, young man, there might be snow on the pumpkin here, but there is still a lot of fire in this old furnace. Much more than you've ever had." His son just shook his head. Willy heard the door open down the hall and stood up. "Here comes your mother-in-law. Stand up and pay her your respects like she deserves."

"No. She's no friendlier to me than you are."

When Willy smiled at her, he had to laugh. Not only did she have a cushioned chair, but she also had someone carrying it for her. This woman, of all the women he knew, had class. Even his own wife, God rest her soul, had always been envious of her class.

"The two of you together in one place? What the hell is going to happen next? Will the walls of hell open and swallow us all up?"

Before he could tell Orval to shut up, Ann did it for him. Elizabeth Jamison, Ann to her friends and family, had always had a quick tongue and a sharp mouth. He just let her have at Orval, as he'd done since his own wife passed on some years ago.

"You are nothing more than a filthy cur, aren't you, Orval Henderson? You'd think that at some point in your misbegotten life you might have gotten a clue on how to treat a woman, and here you sit, in a nasty cell, with your crap lying all around, just as you did at home." She, too, shook her head at him. "No wonder my daughter is happier being divorced from you and living all alone than still shackled to you."

"She was treated like a queen." Ann just tsked at him. "You don't think so? If she were here right now, I'd show you how I treated her. Then I'd have her bail me out of this shithole so that I can go home."

"You've got no home, son. The courts took it a week ago. You don't have a car or a bank account, even though it was empty. Hell, you really didn't have a pot to piss in, even before all this came about. Did anyone ever tell you about taxes, and how they have to be paid or else?" He said that he was above that. "Yes, I can see where that thinking has gotten you right where you need to be. Cameron, he told me that you have been pestering him for months now about giving you money. And my little Caitlynn as well."

"In the event that you've forgotten, Father, she's my daughter, not yours. And she's as ungrateful as her mother and brother. Christ, can't you see what they've done to me? I'm their father, and they're leaving me here to rot. Did you hear about Cameron? He's living with another man. Up to no good too, I'm betting." Willy said that he hoped that they were. "You would. You're as perverted as they are. And Cattie hasn't come to see me once since I've been locked away."

"Caitlynn is in the hospital, last I heard." Orval didn't even ask Ann why, but asked if she had given her any money for him. "No, and I'd not ask her for any, either. She'll be getting married soon, I'm to understand. Met her a very nice cop who rescued her when there was an attempted rape. Tyson had been out doing some undercover work, with Cam's approval, when she was nearly killed. I don't know what we would have done had he not been there. But he's a very nice man, and Cameron, of course, just thinks the world of him."

"Is he going to be screwing him next?" Willy told him to shut up. "No, I will not. I can't stand the fact that he's out there, living it up and having this grand affair, when I'm stuck in here with nothing. I mean, it's bad enough that he's gay, but to rub it in my face, that's another story altogether."

"You don't want your children to be happy, Orval? Christ, I spent my entire life trying to make you happy. But you always managed to find a way to toss it back into my face. I've come to believe that you don't know how to be happy. And when you do have a little money to fill your pockets, you toss that away like it's nothing more than tissue paper you've wiped your ass on." Willy felt his face heat up and told Ann that he was sorry.

"Don't worry about it, Willy. I had it on the tip of my tongue to tell him what I thought. And trust me, yours was much cleaner." He laughed. Willy just couldn't help it. This woman — not that he'd ever asked her age; his own missus had figured it out — was two years older than him. Beautiful, outspoken, and to a point, rude. His Caitlynn had gotten it honestly from her. "Well, I guess we might as well tell him the good news now, don't you think? Then you can take me out to dinner."

Ann stood up, and he did as well. Willy loved her. Not like he had his first wife — no, there was none like his Caitlynne. But he'd fallen in love with Ann as surely as he'd been breathing. And they were going to live together, with his grandchildren right around him. Hopefully, sometime soon, they'd both have a baby to bounce on their knees before they really did keel over.

"Your father and I are going to be whooping it up too, I guess you could say. We've gotten us a nice condo with a single big bed in it. Think about that a moment, Orval. Your father and I having sex in any part of the house we want. And we'll be leaving all our money to your children — not you, but the spawns, as I've heard you call them, that you and your lovely wife created." Orval stood near the bars, staring at both of them. Not just staring, but hatred like he'd never seen before that seemed to be pouring off him. "You can stick that feather in your cap and wear it. Or not. I don't really care, you callous bastard."

After she kissed Willy on the mouth, Ann picked up her chair and left them there. Orval was still staring at her until the door closed behind her. Then he looked at his father.

"You're leaving your money to my kids? Don't you think they both have more than enough? Christ, Dad, what the fuck are they going to do with it? They don't even spend what they have now." He asked him if he'd heard what Ann said about them living together. "I don't care where you live. Maybe if you have enough sex with her, it'll kill you both. Before you change your wills, I hope. You have to leave me something, Dad. I'm your son."

He'd not heard a damned thing but what affected him. Willy was both disappointed and crushed by his son more than he'd ever been. Sitting down on the chair that had been his, he just stared at him. There wasn't any hope for Orval. He was never going to change. It was like he'd raised a toddler—except, Willy thought, by now a toddler would have gotten it.

"You aren't getting anything from us. None of us. Your children, me, Ann, no one. I have never, until this very moment, thought of you as anything but my son. But right now, I'm done with you and your demands." Willy stood up. "I'm to inform you that neither Caitlynn nor Cameron will be by to see you. They're not going to your hearing, and they aren't going to pay anything to make your life better in prison. Nor will I. You've made your bed, several times over, by being a mess, and that is where you'll have to stay. As of this very minute, Orval, I'm washing my hands of you. Do not call me or anyone I love again. Understand me?"

"You have to leave me something, old man. You do know that I'm your son."

Willy picked up his chair. He was walking down the hall, his heart breaking, when something hit him in the back of the head. It took him to the floor, the blood on his hand scaring him a little.

"Did you hear me? I said I'm your son. You have to do something about this."

Getting up was more difficult than he thought it should have been. Using the chair as a crutch, he made it to the door, his son screaming at him to come back the entire time. By the time Willy made it through the door, he knew that he was going to be all right, but he was hurt well beyond the injury to his head. His heart was broken.

Willy let Ann fuss over him—it was nice after what had just happened. Then he let them call an ambulance. Jake, a friend of his grandson's, said it would be better for the state of mind of Orval. He told him that he didn't have any state of mind but how it would benefit him.

"Yes, well, he's proven that over and over. You know, Mr. Henderson?" He told him to call him Willy. "All right, Willy. I think I could make a very good living as an attorney with this family, don't you think?"

They were still laughing when the medics came in. They said he'd need stitches and an x-ray. At his age, they didn't want to take any chances. Orval had attempted murder—he'd thrown a steak knife from the tray at him, to add to the long list of crap he'd done.

His family, extended and all, were there waiting for him when he got to the hospital. Willy hugged them all several times. He'd just witnessed an act of a madman that was his son, and he needed the little extra hugs and kisses. Lying there, waiting for someone to take him down for the x-ray, he told Jake what had happened. It was hurtful to tell it again—thinking about it all had just about done him in.

He was turned this way and that, everyone being so careful with his old bones, and then brought to his room. Willy told them to have some dinner, bring him back a little something when they returned, and they left. Then he was in a wheelchair, alone with his granddaughter and her new love, Tyson.

"I have something to tell you, old man." He took her hand in his and kissed the back of it. "I love you as well. But I have to tell you something, and I want you to listen to me. Understand?"

"You act more and more like Ann every day. Has anyone

183

pointed that out to you before?" She said that they had. Then Tyson left them for a moment when his phone rang. "You're in love. It looks good on you."

"I am in love, but don't change the subject. I want you to know that you are a part of our family. And thus, you're an immortal." He shook his head. "Yes, you are. And I expect you to stay here from now on, sexing it up with Grandma Ann, who I think loves you too. I need you around so that you can sit with my children, hold me when I need it, and just be the annoying old man that I know you are all the time."

"What a thing to say to me." He laughed when she did. "Really? We're immortals? Both Ann and I?"

"Yes. I don't care if it's all right or not, but if it's not, you have to tell me why. I want to fix it so that you'll be happy being here." Willy told her that having family around him made anything worthwhile. "Good. And the money that you were going to leave for Cam and I? I want you and Grandma Ann to spend it on something foolish. Something fun for the two of you. You're going to be around for a very long time, Grandda, and you can always make more or get some from me and Cam. We have plenty to share with you."

"I love you, Caitlynn, my dear. You and Cameron are the best possible thing that could have happened to me." She kissed him on the cheek. "Tyson, he going to change you soon? I don't have to tell you that you'll feel better when you do."

"We've talked about that, and children. We're going to have some as soon as I go into heat, what his kind calls it. I love you, Grandda, with all my heart." He asked her how much did Tyson have. "As much as you'll allow him to have."

Willy was sitting in the dark when Ann came in to be with him. She climbed into his bed, put her head on his chest, and cried a little. He let her, then asked her what had happened.

"That person hurt you." So, he thought, Orval was just going to be that person to them. He liked it and told her that. "Yes, well, if we're going to be babysitting, we—or at least I—will have to clean up my fucking language."

They were both still laughing when the nurse came in to check on them. Willy was in love, for the second time in his life, and he was going to be around long enough to see his great-grandchildren, as well as beyond. Life was good.

~*~

Cam loved his new position. He was still having issues with some of the thoughts that his agents had, but he was learning quickly, how to sort them out into things that he should worry about and things that he should not. And thanks to Rick, he was in love with his office too.

"I guess what they say about gays having good fashion sense is true." Cattie sat across from him when she entered his office. "I wanted to tell you first—I'm going to give up the stationhouse job. And Tyson is going to take it. I think you might have known that when you sent him here, didn't you?"

"I knew that he'd be a good help for you. But no, I had no idea that he'd be your mate. You're happy, aren't you, Cattie?" She grinned, and that was about as telling as it got. "I'm so happy for you both. When am I going to be an uncle?"

"In about ten months." He asked her if she was serious. "Sort of. He wants to change me first, and we're hoping by the first cycle I have, I'll be in heat. I've been to the doctor, and he said that I'm healthy for both. And that buddy of Jake's is going to be here in a few days. I guess he's taking his little boy on a trip first. He's a good doctor too, and Jake has all but convinced him that he needs to stay, which I guess he's thinking hard about it."

"Good. A little boy, huh? I guess he's been married?" She

told him how Forrest was handling his divorce from a real bitch. "One of those, huh? Well, that's fine. And you'll be the first I tell that Rick and I have decided to adopt. Forrest is helping out with that too. Jake said that it's easier to have an attorney helping rather than looking on our own."

They talked about this and that. Thanksgiving was next month, and they were trying to figure out if there were any traditions that they'd be involved in. Cattie told him that none of them had come from a good home, and she was going to suggest that they make it up as they go along.

"I think we should let Grandda and Grandma Ann do it if no one has any objections. They've been around the longest, were the happiest before their other half left them, and now have found each other. Maybe they'd have some way of gathering us all together under one roof so we can be a true family." She asked him if he and Rick were coming over for dinner tonight. "Yes. We have to celebrate my sister being released from the hospital, and an upcoming wedding."

"Nothing much of a wedding. We're going to keep it low-key. He has some things he has to take care of at his home. Oh, I've taken my house off the market. Tyson and I are going to live there." He told her that was a wonderful idea. "I thought so as well. He loves it, and I really hated to give it up after I thought about it. Do you like him?"

The question startled him, but he smiled at her, asking her why she cared. She started to pace his office and he just let her. When she settled down again, he answered her question with a query of his own.

"While I don't understand why you'd care if I like him, I do. Very much so. And the fact that he saved you from a lot of pain and heartbreak with what happened on the trail gives him big points too. You loving him is also a good point in his corner." She nodded but didn't look convinced. "What is it?"

"I was afraid that it came on too fast. I mean, that night, the first night after it happened, I told him that I loved him. Then I had to wonder if I loved him or was grateful to him for saving my ass. Which he did." Cam said that he knew that. "Do you love Rick? I mean, the love him forever and will never fall out of love with him kind of love?"

He got it then. "Cattie, you and Tyson are mates, just as Rick and I are. Jake and Forrest, as well as Henry and Paddy. Mates, they mate for life. There is nothing that can ever come between them. And nothing will come between the two of you." She nodded. "Did you talk to Tyson about this? I mean, tell him how you feel?"

"I did, and you want to know what he said? Whether or not I ever come to love him as much as he does me, what I have will be enough to keep his heart beating for a very long time." She snorted. "He's such a romantic. Sometimes I just don't know how to react to it."

"You let him pamper you. Let him show you what it's like to be loved by someone other than me. He'll never hurt you. Never treat you with anything but respect and kindness." He watched her nod again. "No, Cattie, those aren't just words, but the truth. You can bank on it."

"What if he turns out like Dad?" *Ah*, he thought. *There is the real reason behind this.* "He might. Mom said that Dad wasn't too bad when they first got together."

"Because our grandparents were giving him anything that he wanted until they finally said no. Then he became the nightmare that he is. And so you know, Grandda disowned him this afternoon. He called in his own lawyer and had the paperwork drawn up. Dad will find out tomorrow before he's taken to court." Cattie asked him this time if he was serious.

"Yes. I found out when I felt Grandda's pain. You'd not believe how much it broke his heart to do that. But he did try and kill him."

"Yes, I couldn't believe that. I guess you're right. Dad has been and always will be a fundamental asshole that should have been left to the side of the road the day we were born. I think that was when Mom did it. Pushed him away." Cam knew that there was more than that as to why his mom had pushed Dad away, but he didn't tell Cattie. "All right. I guess that I can categorically say that Tyson isn't like our dad. But I still worry."

"I really think you should talk to Tyson. Tell him what you think, where you're coming from. It might make you see that he has nothing but your best at heart." Cattie said that she would. "No. Do it. I think— I can check to see what he thinks about this, but I believe it would be better if he told you himself, Cattie. The man is so in love with you. Just like Grandda is with Grandma Ann."

"Now that is a match that I have no questions about." She was laughing when she stood up. "You're right. I'm going to talk to Tyson today. He has something planned for tonight, and before I see what it is, I'm going to see what he thinks about my insecurities. And I have a lot of them, too."

He thought that they both did, and they stemmed mostly from their father. Closing up his office, he made sure that everything was off and locked up. Not that he didn't trust the one on the door—he'd had it especially put in when he took over—but there were things in here that he'd just as soon keep to himself. Like the things that Rick had left him in the way of funny mementos.

They'd taken a small weekend vacation a few days ago and had bought some Christmas gifts. Not too many, but they also got themselves some silly and not so silly things that they loved. Personal items that Cam knew he'd treasure forever. And then there was the picture of the two of them that was on his desk.

They'd been coming out of a restaurant, holding hands and having fun, when this little girl, probably no more than about fourteen or so, asked if she could snap their picture — for ten dollars, she'd told them. Not only had she really sent it to their email address when asked, but she took them up on staying at a hotel — not the one they were in — and having a few meals delivered to her. She was, they found out, nineteen and terrified. They were going to go and see about talking her into coming to work for them in a couple of weeks. Rick had told him today that she was still at the hotel, and still being careful she wasn't trapped someplace. Cam knew for a fact that her father was looking for her, and that she'd been abused, physically, for several months before she'd been able to run.

"We'll bring her back with us this time. I think that she'd make a great nanny for the kids." They'd talked about adopting at great length and had decided that they didn't care about the age or sex, but that they someday wanted to raise a baby, if they could. "She said that she has a good education. And I know that you've checked everything out."

"I did." He looked at Rick. "She might not like kids, did you think of that?" He just snorted at him. "All right, know it all, how do you know that?"

"She likes animals. And babies aren't that much different than say, a puppy, right?"

They were still laughing about that when they drove home the next day. It was going to be nice having someone they could depend on to watch the children, but Cam thought they should get some first. Yes, he thought as he locked his car at home, life was going to be an adventure from now on, and he could not

189

wait to see what was in store for them all.

Before You Go...

HELP AN AUTHOR

write a review

THANK YOU!

Share your voice and help guide other readers to these wonderful books. Even if it's only a line or two your reviews help readers discover the author's books so they can continue creating stories that you'll love. Login to your favorite retailer and leave a review. Thank you.

AWARD WINNING, BESTSELLING AUTHOR

Kathi Barton, winner of the Pinnacle Book Achievement award as well as a best-selling author on Amazon and All Romance books, lives in Nashport, Ohio with her husband Paul. When not creating new worlds and romance, Kathi and her husband enjoy camping and going to auctions. She can also be seen at county fairs with her husband who is an artist and potter.

Her muse, a cross between Jimmy Stewart and Hugh Jackman, brings her stories to life for her readers in a way that has them coming back time and again for more. Her favorite genre is paranormal romance with a great deal of spice. You can visit Kathi online and drop her an email if you'd like. She loves hearing from her fans. aaronskiss@gmail.com.

Follow Kathi on her blog: http://kathisbartonauthor.blogspot.com/